BE CAREFUL WHAT YOU WISH FOR

LORRAINE MURPHY

INKUBATOR
BOOKS

Published by Inkubator Books
www.inkubatorbooks.com

Copyright © 2023 by Lorraine Murphy

Lorraine Murphy has asserted her right to be identified as the author of this work.

ISBN (eBook): 978-1-83756-174-2
ISBN (Paperback): 978-1-83756-175-9
ISBN (Hardback): 978-1-83756-176-6

PROLOGUE

She fights for breath. My next move will decide if she lives or dies.

I thought I'd be compelled to help in the face of death, that my natural empathy would have kicked in and I'd have switched to automatic action mode, calling an ambulance or performing CPR. Anything except sitting here, watching her gasp for breath, doing nothing.

I am not a killer; this is not murder. If – when – she dies without my intervention, it is nature's wish. No court in the land will convict me if they discover what happened. Not that they will.

The crying stops and her breath becomes more laboured. I should do something right about now, but I don't see the point. She's more value to me dead than alive. If I help her, she could ruin everything, and if I don't, my secrets go with her to the grave and all my wishes come true.

With one final moan she's gone. Her spirit leaves her body, her face is transformed. She is a peaceful, serene woman, not the lowlife she was.

I put my ear to her mouth. Nothing.

They say death is the final leveller, but I disagree. I think it's the final lie. No matter what terrible things you've done in your life, they fix your hair and make-up, dress you up in your Sunday best and parade you out for people to eulogise about you.

What will they say about her? She was a lady, a lovely woman, kept herself to herself. They might even praise her parenting skills. That's a laugh.

They won't tell the truth, that she was a selfish and weak human being who put her own interests ahead of her child's, again and again. She wasn't fit to carry the name "Mother".

There'll be an autopsy, no doubt, where they'll pronounce her death as natural, not suspicious. The funeral will follow and the priest will offer the usual platitudes. She was taken too soon, it was a terrible loss for the family. Blah blah blah. All lies.

I lift the sheet and cover her face, with no concern for leaving fingerprints. This is no crime scene; there will be no investigation.

Is it murder, letting someone die when you could save them? I don't think so. Not that it matters how I think.

Either way, she's dead.

1

TARA

Tuesday, 8 November

Tara Ryan was fine. Tickety boo. Working nine to five weekdays, doing chores on Saturdays, and sleeping late on Sundays. Life was easy, but no matter the day, dinner was at 6:30 p.m. sharp with Mary, her elderly mother.

With a roof over her head, no financial worries and someone who loved her more than anything in the whole wide world, she was lucky. True, Tara Ryan's life was also boring, humdrum and dreary, but it was fine. Until that rainy evening when she opened that email.

Dark well before 5:30 p.m., the icy rain lashed down on Tara as she ran from work to catch the train to her mother's house. She jostled for space on the packed platform at Grand Canal Dock. As the train entered the station, she stood tall, preparing for the nightly push, every man and

woman out for themselves on Dublin Rail. The carriage
doors opened, people poured in and she spotted it – a vacant
seat on the far-left side of the carriage. She made a beeline
for it, but a suited man pushed by her, knocking her against
another commuter, and took the seat for himself.

"Who said chivalry is dead?" Tara muttered under her
breath, and held the handle on the seat above his head. She
glanced around – all the same faces, taking the same trip at
the same time every night. Standing room only, glued to
their phones, some laughing to themselves, others on calls,
but all ignoring each other. Not that she was judging; she
was usually found deep in her phone too, but she was tired
tonight. Instead, she looked at the window that reflected
back the distracted commuters in the carriage and zoned out
until, twenty-seven minutes later, the familiar announce-
ment on the tannoy brought her back.

The next stop is Cushla, Cois an Lae. Please mind the gap.

The second the doors opened, the sea air rushed in. In
automatic mode, she alighted with the same people she'd
boarded with that morning, still miles away in her own
thoughts when someone pushed from behind, thrusting her
forward. Tara stumbled, trying to grab the person in front,
but they turned left and she plunged head first into the
green wooden fence, landing on the ground in a massive
puddle. Her backpack bounced from her shoulder onto the
platform as the doors of the train closed and its red and
yellow lights disappeared down the track. Men and women
rushed by her, not one offering to help, intent on getting
home to their real lives, with people who they actually
cared for. Within minutes, the station was deserted and Tara
got to her feet. She brushed herself off and retrieved her
backpack, now filthy and wet, then crossed over the pedes-

trian bridge, through the turnstile and onto the road outside.

The wind rose up from the Irish Sea, whipping her greying curly hair into her face. Her long, brown skirt blew up to reveal fleece leggings. She thanked God her fellow commuters were gone ahead as she tried to hold her skirt with one hand and the hood of her black padded coat with the other hand, now stinging from the fall.

At the top of the hill, she turned right and the rain pelted against her. How she wished she had an umbrella. She always carried one, but a colleague had borrowed hers today at lunchtime and Tara knew that was the last she'd see of it. They always took them, the glam squad at work, but never returned them. Not to worry, look on the bright side – umbrellas blew inside out more often than not in this seaside town and in a few minutes' time she'd be warm and cosy and tucking into a hearty meal. What day was it again? Ah yes, Tuesday.

Counting her blessings to distract herself from her now throbbing knee, she started with mobility. Mother would say how lucky she was to have the use of her legs, that was blessing number one. Number two, she was in the full of her health, which was quite the feat, considering everything.

She turned left by the church, deep in thought, searching for number three, and then screamed as a car sped by, planing straight through the flooded roadside and drenching her from head to toe. She hurried around the corner away from the traffic, the freezing water trickling down her back. It was then she heard the waves.

Living here for her entire life, Tara was almost immune to the sound of the Irish Sea, but tonight it was much louder than usual. A storm was most certainly on the way, although she didn't remember them giving that on last night's weather forecast. Then again, she tended to drift off during the news that mother insisted she watch with her. Every. Single. Night. In two minutes, she'd be there. Walking down the hill of multicoloured houses towards the harbour. She returned to her blessings; where was she? Oh yes, three – living so close to the station, although a car would be nice for wet nights like this. Her mother would be appalled at her laziness, but she had nothing to worry about. Tara couldn't drive. She had floated the idea of getting driving lessons once, but her mother shot it down, after what had happened to Daddy RIP. Her breath caught – Daddy. Long gone, always missed.

A yellow house still had its Halloween decorations up, while there was a Christmas tree in the window of the adjoining pink house. November was far too early to put the Christmas tree up, but she knew what Daddy would say – it's never too early to celebrate and feel happy. He loved Christmas, everything about it. It wasn't something they celebrated since he left. It was too painful.

By the time Tara reached her mother's terraced house, she was soaked, shivering and ravenous. The wind whipped her hair into her face and she could barely see to get the key in the front door, but, when she did, a wall of heat rushed out to meet her. She stepped into the narrow hallway, with its orange patterned carpet and floral wallpaper, and her soul calmed at the familiar smell ... ah, Tuesday. She loved Tuesday. Tuesday was stew day.

"Is that you, Tara pet?" her mother called from the living room, the theme tune to *The Evening Show* blaring from the old TV.

"Yes, Mother, it's me. Terrible night out there." Tara spread her coat along the white radiator in the hall and unlaced her black boots while Snowy, her mother's favourite cat, watched from his wicker basket.

"Good girl," her mother called back. "It gave rain this afternoon on the forecast; there's a storm on the way. I hope you had an umbrella with you."

Tara took a deep breath, counted to five, then entered the sitting room. The open fire blazed up the yellow brick chimney. Sooty, their oldest cat and Tara's favourite of the three, lay fast asleep on the mat. She'd found him in the garden as a tiny kitten, cornered by a hissing Snowy. She coaxed Snowy inside and the kitten scarpered, but the next morning he was back. She fed him and soon he was a regular guest in the house, and although Snowy was unimpressed, he'd accepted this new housemate. Mother always said that Sooty rescued Tara, not the other way around. Down the end of the long room, Marmalade sat on the dinner table where her mother set cutlery out. Now there was a cat who did what she wanted, when she wanted. The table was far too big for two people, yet her mother insisted they eat there every evening.

Tara kept her head down as she passed the brass mirror over the fireplace and kissed her mother on the cheek. "You look well," she said. "That stew smells gorgeous. I'm starving."

Her mother tutted. "You are not *starving*. You are *hungry*. I didn't give the best years of my life to teaching for you to disrespect language." She looked up and stopped mid-sentence. "What on earth happened to you? You're bleeding!"

Tara touched her cheek and examined her hand, to find blood on her fingers. "I fell getting off the train but I'm grand. I didn't realise I'd cut myself."

Her mother sat back in her wheelchair and drank her in from head to toe, her crooked mouth hanging open. "Good Lord, Tara pet, you look awful, like something the cat dragged in. Go on out to the bathroom and clean yourself up while I dish up the dinner."

Tara did what she was told, washing her face in the sink of the adapted downstairs bathroom. She returned, lifted the cat off the table and selected a roll.

"You were always the same, a real Clumsy Carol," her mother called from the kitchen. "Always falling over your own feet. Always a worry for me."

"Thanks for coming, Tara," Tara muttered under her breath. "Very good of you to give up your evening, Tara. I appreciate it, Tara."

"What's that?"

"Nothing, Mother."

"You're very good for coming over," her mother said, as the timer on the oven beeped. *Like I have a choice*, Tara thought, and went out to help, returning with a steaming pot of stew and laying it on the metal stand. She took the lid off the pot and inhaled the delicious smell. Beef stew. Steak, onions, potatoes, carrots and celery, far too much food for the two of them, but after one spoon of the hot brown stock, Tara knew she'd demolish it like she always did. Her mother was the best cook in Ireland. She was also the holiest, which Tara was reminded of when she cleared her throat and eyeballed the soup spoon halfway into Tara's mouth. Tara put it down and joined her hands.

Her mother bowed her head. "Bless Us O Lord, for these thy gifts which we are about to receive from thy bounty, through Christ Our Lord, Amen."

"Amen," Tara repeated. She dipped her bread roll into the stew and took a bite, careful not to burn her mouth.

"How's work?" Mary asked.

"Good!" she replied, avoiding eye contact.

Her mother took a trembling spoon to her own tiny portion, more suited to a baby bird than an eighty-two-year-old woman, and chose a tiny chunk of beef. She raised it to her mouth, then ground it between her four remaining front teeth – two on the top and two on the bottom. She refused to wear her dentures; said they were a nuisance, and besides, nobody saw her these days except for Tara and Doctor Lucas.

Tara dug into the stew as Mary chewed that one piece of meat, the only other sound the brass clock ticking on the wall. That clock had tormented her as a child, waiting for time to pass in Mother's home school.

"Sorry," Tara said. "I should have asked. How was your day? Any news?"

Mary wiped her mouth with her napkin and brushed a wisp of white hair from her face. "I'm an old housebound woman, what news would I have? I made some scones. You can take them home with you, share them with your new friend. What was her name? Joan, was it?" She sat forward, awaiting information, any information.

"Yes, that's right. It's Joan."

"How is she, love?"

"She's good," Tara said, and continued to eat.

"Ah, come on," Mary said when it was obvious nothing else was coming. "Give me some bit of news."

Tara put her spoon down and patted her mouth with her napkin. "Okay, well, do you remember I told you about Joan

and the DNA test she did? Today the results came in and—"
Tara leaned in closer for dramatic effect.

"Elbows, love."

"Sorry." Tara put her arms down by her side. "As I was saying, today the results came in and you'll never believe this – the man Joan was dating, her boyfriend Tommy, is her second cousin! What are the chances?"

Mary Ryan had two ways of reacting to a story. One, when she liked it, her blue eyes would sparkle and she'd nod for Tara to continue. The other, which she was doing now, was to sit back in her chair and cross her arms, and this was usually followed by a list of her concerns.

"Obviously she broke up with him," Tara said, trying to head her off at the pass, but it was too late.

"Your generation are so obsessed with knowing everything. Dig, dig, dig. Why can't you leave well enough alone?" Mary said. "Was it expensive, the DNA test?"

"I didn't ask her how much she paid." Tara's palms moistened and she picked at the old scab on the back of her hand. "And what does that matter anyway? She discovered her boyfriend is her cousin. What if she'd never found out and married him?"

Mary shrugged. "In our day that happened all the time, cousin marrying cousin, and there was nothing wrong with us, plus isn't it good enough for royalty? Where ignorance is bliss it's a folly to be wise, if you ask me."

"Yes, Mother," Tara said. "I suppose you're right." There was no point in arguing with an old woman; it was like fighting with your reflection.

The oven pinged. Saved by the bell. Mary went out to the kitchen, returning with a steaming tart in a tea towel. "Apple, your favourite!"

She said that every night too, but in fairness, she was right. Apple tart was Tara's favourite, especially with the special ice cream that Mary scooped on top.

It was a mutually beneficial arrangement. As Mary's only child, Tara called every night to look after the things her mother couldn't do for herself since the accident and brought her news from the world outside. In return, Mary looked after her, and this included making dinner. Tara sipped her water. She would have enjoyed a glass of something stronger now and again, but Mary's table never had alcohol. Not since the Christmas Eve crash all those years ago that killed Daddy RIP and left her mother paralysed from the waist down. The judge said the driver was three times over the limit before sentencing him to two prison sentences to run concurrently. That man served eighteen years before he walked free, despite hundreds of letters from Mary begging the authorities to keep him locked up. On the day he was released, Mary sobbed. "He's free to live his life while your father is dead and I'm stuck in this chair, in this purgatory. He destroyed our lives. Only for you, Tara, I'd be lost."

Tara polished off the tart and sat back, full as a tick. "I'll help you clean up."

"Sit down and relax," Mary said. "I'm more than capable. Besides, what will I do with myself all day tomorrow? Leave me at least something to occupy myself."

Doctor Lucas said it was good for Mary to keep active as long as she was able, and who was Tara to argue? Besides, it suited her to the ground, hating as she did housework of any description. Saturday was her least favourite day of the week.

Mary returned with a pot of tea, which Tara poured into

two china cups, adding milk to Mary's and leaving her own black. She carried them through to the living room and handed one to her mother, who was in situ, awaiting the main evening news to start. Tara took her place in the mustard velvet armchair to the right of her mother, as the familiar jingle finished and the blonde newsreader began.

Tonight, on the main evening news: House prices are set to hike again for the third month in a row, a man is found murdered in Cork and parents are back in the high court as new allegations come to light in the Cherish the Child children's home scandal.

Mary increased the volume so much it hurt Tara's ears. She was particularly interested in this developing story, growing up in Mayo herself.

It is one week since whistle-blower Breda Burke came forward and allegations against the Cherish the Child children's home in Lenburgh, County Mayo, continued today, with more people coming forward to tell their story.

An older woman with short, brown hair and bags under her eyes filled the TV screen.

It was human trafficking, pure and simple. Children, babies, taken from young unmarried mothers like myself and sold to the highest bidder. Someone must be held accountable.

The newsreader returned.

Gardai says they are making substantial progress, but with the destruction of the majority of the home's records in a freak fire last year, it will be difficult. They are asking anyone affected to get in touch.

Mary was glued to the TV, as she was every night.

In other news, property prices will continue to increase until supply increases substantially, according to Housing Ireland. In its latest housing market monitor, it says soaring rents are pushing more people to want to purchase, which will keep upward pressure on prices even as the economy slows. But with the average price of a house in Ireland now over seven times the average wage, becoming a houseowner is something most people can merely dream about.

How lucky Tara was to have her own place, with no mortgage to pay. She looked at her white-haired mother, tiny in her chair, and her heart filled with gratitude. So what if this was all she had; she was utterly blessed and she knew it.

At 9:30 p.m., after the weather forecast, which confirmed an impending storm but promised a brighter day for Wednesday, Tara drew the lilac floral curtains in the downstairs bedroom. Mary changed into her nightdress and Tara emptied her colostomy bag in the adjacent wet room, then helped her into bed and performed the nightly colonic irrigation, which Doctor Lucas recommended to keep Mary comfortable. Tara reckoned it was a job for a professional carer but there was no way of saying that without hurting her mother's feelings. Instead, she performed the same duties every night, then tucked her mother into the bed. Snowy jumped up beside her, ready to snuggle in for the night.

"Goodnight, Tara love."

"Goodnight, Mother. See you tomorrow."

"Please, God. And, Tara, I do love you. You know that, don't you? I'd be lost without you."

"I know, Mother, and I love you too. I'd be as lost without you." Tara kissed her on her cheek, then set about looking after the other two cats. She sat on the kitchen floor and they came, curling around her and rubbing against her hands. She scooped cat food onto their plates, poured milk into their bowls, cleared out the litter trays and switched off all the lights except for the one on the landing. Mary insisted it gave the impression that someone was upstairs. She looked in on her mother one final time, so small she barely made a bump under the duvet. Blowing a kiss, she left, pulling the front door behind her.

Outside, the rain was pelting down and the wind howled. The waves roared in the distance. Three minutes would take her home, if she turned right out the garden gate, right again at the end of the residential street and crossed the coast road to her gated complex. Tara pulled up her hood and turned left, towards the neon lights of the convenience store, 24/7, at the end of the street. There, she filled a basket with essentials and went through the self-checkout, feeling invisible to the young shop assistant who sat swiping on his phone. With two plastic shopping bags and a heavy heart, Tara went home, alone, to her penthouse apartment.

Mary said she was very good for coming, but the truth was she had nowhere else to be. With her mother's declining health, and latest diagnosis, she was so very lonely and petrified for her future.

"Idyllic, but expensive, with a stunning view," the over-confident estate agent with the slicked back hair claimed when she'd first viewed her apartment. "Ideal for a young couple starting out."

"I'm on my own," she'd answered, which drew him closer. Too close.

"Is that right?" he'd asked. "We have other properties I could show you. Maybe we could discuss it over coffee sometime?"

Tara had walked away from him, but he followed her up the wooden step of the split-level apartment and into the ceiling-to-floor windows that framed the whole corner of the open-plan living area. To her left, multicoloured fishing boats bobbed in the harbour and straight ahead the Irish Sea stretched to the horizon. It was beautiful, but the only view she cared about was to her right, the back of Mary's house. Tara could keep an eye on her from here, and in that moment, with this man standing far too close to her, Mary could return the favour.

"So, how about that date?" he asked.

Tara had waved, pretending to see her. "There's Mother."

He'd recoiled. "Mother? Wow, talk about staying close to home. That'll cramp your style." He looked her up and down in slow motion. "A fine-looking woman like you."

"I'll take it." Tara had handed him the deposit cheque, signed by Mary. That was almost twenty years ago, and he was the last man, with the exception of tradesmen, to set foot in her apartment.

Undoing the top, middle and bottom deadlocks, she opened her door and switched on the light. Dirty dishes lay on the counter ahead, where she left them that morning, the duvet from last night was still on the couch with a half-eaten bowl of cereal on a stool in front of it. An empty Club orange bottle and a popcorn bag were strewn on the floor. She switched off the light. Saturday was the day for housework and that wasn't for another four days. In the dark, she stepped onto the upper level of the apartment and gazed out over the harbour. The view was magnificent, distant houses twinkling like fairy lights against the darkness, or stars against the sky. When she first moved in, she'd flash the living room lights twice to let Mary know she was home safe and Mary would flash them back, but they stopped doing that when the house was burgled while her mother slept. Luckily, the intruders only took cash and jewellery, but it rattled her mother so much she seemed to age overnight.

The Gardai said it was likely someone was watching, as they seemed to know exactly where to look to find the items.

In the master bedroom, Tara took off her turtleneck and long skirt, dropping them onto the biscuit carpet beside the other clothes. That was the best thing about living on your own. You could leave things wherever you got the notion to. In pyjamas, housecoat and slippers, she sauntered back to the kitchen, poured a glass of white and took it to the table in the bay window. She switched on her laptop and opened her emails. Ads, ads and more ads. The commercial hype of the run into Christmas every year the same, selling stuff she neither wanted nor needed.

Daddy would have loved to be here.

She deleted email after email but then one caught her eye.

Tara Ryan: Your MyFamily results are in!

What she hadn't told her mother earlier was that Joan was not her friend, she was her supervisor, who she'd overheard saying she'd ordered a DNA test a few weeks ago.

As an introverted, shy, odd person, call it what you want, and many had, Tara struggled in company and never knew what to say, which normally meant saying the wrong thing or nothing at all. All she'd ever wanted was to be normal, but following the goings-on of last summer, Tara promised herself she would make friends; she would push herself out of her comfort zone and talk to people. She ordered the DNA test online the same night Joan mentioned it; maybe it would give her something to talk about in the canteen, if anyone ever bothered to speak to her.

When Mother asked earlier about the price of the DNA

test, Tara knew exactly how much it cost. €100. She knew because she had paid it too.

She stared at the email from MyFamily.com.

It invited, flashing yellow and blue.

Click to discover your DNA results!

She hesitated. What if she discovered something like Joan had? What if ... oh, what was she talking about? Her life was fine, blessed for sure, about as interesting as watching the sport results after the main evening news. She held her breath and wished for some excitement, then clicked the button.

DNA Matches: 122 fourth cousins or closer. View all matches?

What harm could it do? If she discovered family abroad, she could go visit, finally getting on an aeroplane. *What about Mother?* She could have so much in common with her cousins, perhaps they'd visit Ireland too. It was never realistic to expect her colleagues, with their manicured nails and fashionable clothes, to hang out, but there was surely someone out there amongst the billions of people on the planet who would. She clicked the link.

Close Family: Cassandra Blake: Full match.

Full blood relative: Parent, child or sibling of the same parents.

2

TARA

Wednesday, 9 November

Tara's alarm woke her up. It was morning, but it took a moment to figure out where she was. She opened one eye and found her phone. 7:10 a.m. She pressed snooze, lay back and was drifting back to sleep when BOOM – the memory of last night made her jolt upright in her bed. The DNA results!

It had been all hours when she got to sleep. All night she investigated, starting with reading the FAQs on the site.

So, you've discovered a full match. What does it mean?

A full match means you are directly related. This is a full parent, child or sibling relationship.

This woman Tara had never heard of was her mother,

sister or child?! It made no sense. She knew her mother: Mary Ryan. She didn't have, or want, a child of her own, ever, and there were no sisters, although she'd always wished for one. Ever since she was small, she'd plagued her mother for a sister but never got one.

She scrambled to find out more about this mystery woman on the MyFamily site, but her profile was locked. Tara couldn't see anything but the woman's name, not even a photograph. She googled her, searched for her on social media, but there was nothing. Back on the MyFamily site, she noticed an envelope in the bottom right corner of the screen – send private message.

Tara clicked it and started to type. She typed and deleted, typed and deleted, ranging from asking lots of questions and saying too much to eventually settling on:

Dear Cassandra,

I hope you are well. My name is Tara Ryan and I see we are full matches on MyFamily. If you could get in touch with me to discuss, I would greatly appreciate it.

Kind regards,
Tara Ryan

She considered including her phone number but decided against it, then took a deep breath and clicked send. She waited, and waited, but no reply came. The sound of traffic lessened on the coast road outside and the wind died down. She refilled her glass and, losing patience, sent another message.

Dear Cassandra,

*It's Tara again. Apologies for another email but I really
need to talk to you. Can you please answer my message? I
have no idea how we can be related and it's driving me
crazy.*

Kind regards,
Tara.

Still nothing. Tara scoured the internet again. She tried
searching for every form of her name.

Cassandra Blake
Cassie Blake
Sandra Blake
Sandy Blake

But her searches yielded no results.

The alarm went off again. Tara dragged herself out of
bed and into the hot shower. She chose a sports bra and full
briefs from her white wooden chest of drawers, then opened
the wardrobe to create an outfit from the three folded piles.
A flecked woollen skirt from the left pile, brown leggings
from the middle and a darker brown polo-neck from the pile
to the right. She dried off her long hair enough to get the wet
out, packed Mary's cherry scones into her backpack and
pulled on her brown flat boots. Grabbing her coat, she set
her security alarm, locked the door and left her apartment
for the 8 a.m. train.

Outside, the sky was clear and the sun was out, the overturned wheelie bins and swirling litter the only proof of the

previous night's storm. Tara tapped her annual ticket at the entrance of Cushla station, the barrier lifted and she took her usual place on the busy platform, determined not to be pushed aside again. She touched her face to find the wound already scabbed over. She should have checked herself in the mirror before she left but her mind was all over the place.

A full match.

The train arrived four minutes later, already wedged with people, and Tara was pushed by her fellow commuters and into the middle of the carriage. Her head spun and she reached for the closest handle, as the train left the station for Dublin city centre. Along with almost every other person on the train, she checked her phone. No emails.

She switched on her notifications, not wanting to miss any replies from the mysterious Cassandra Blake.

Cassandra Blake.

The train veered right and shook as it changed track, making her stomach lurch. A familiar face approached. Barry, her manager, or Baldy Barry, as they called him in the office. She smiled to be polite, then looked out the window at the new apartment blocks being built and cranes rising high against the skyline. She thought he'd take the hint that she didn't want to talk, but he continued towards her, weaving between the many people who tutted and sighed.

"Tara! Fancy meeting you here! How's it going?"

"Fine," she replied.

He manoeuvred himself until he was standing facing her. "Good, good, that's good. Not so great a morning for me – I'd normally drive into the office but I'd terrible car trouble this morning, bloody thing wouldn't start, so here I am with the great unwashed ha ha."

A tall man standing opposite threw him a look that could kill and coughed.

Barry leaned in closer to her and whispered in a minty breath, "I'll have to watch what I'm saying, otherwise I'll be lynched, eh? Am I right? Eh? Eh?"

Tara couldn't help but grin. "Probably best alright."

"Do you take the train every morning?" The train jolted and his hand brushed off hers, softer than she'd expected, and warmer too. Pink, like his happy face, now awaiting an answer.

"Yes, I take the train every morning. I don't drive."

His blue eyes twinkled. "Sure, I'm two stations up the road from you, I could swing by and give you a lift when my car is fixed, save you having to travel with this lot." He looked up to the tall man and made a face.

Tara grinned.

"What do you say I pick you up—" he started.

"No, thanks. I prefer the train," she said, cutting him off at the pass. Better to be upfront with these things.

The whole bottom half of his face flushed like he'd been dipped in strawberry jam. "Okay, no problem. Your call, I respect that. Boundaries, consent and all that. By the way, the guys from the office are going for drinks on Saturday evening in Brooke's to celebrate my big five-oh. I'm sure you got the email."

It was her turn to feel the heat. "Um, no, I didn't get any email."

His face turned into a whole strawberry. "Oh, sorry, it was supposed to be sent to the whole department. Anyway, consider this your invitation. I'd love if you could make it. Brooke's, Saturday night. Eight until late. Be there or be square." He shot two imaginary guns at her.

Tara froze. "No, thanks," was all she could manage. She swore no more work parties after the last time.

The rest of the journey was as awkward as it was stomach-churning and Tara barely managed to swipe into the ground-floor office of Partners Plus Ltd before emptying the contents of her stomach in one of their luxury toilets. She washed her hands in a white marble sink and examined her reflection in the mirrored wall. Frizzy hair hung past her shoulders, lifeless and dull. Her face was round yet simultaneously drawn, huge bags hung under her brown eyes, and her cheek was grazed and bruised. With hips that were widening by the day, Mother was right – she was like something the cat dragged in. Maybe it was as well this Cassandra Blake didn't reply, whoever she was. Who would want to be related to this?

She checked her phone. No new emails.

Every morning for the last twenty-two years, Tara started her day in Partners Plus at the coffee dock. She located her mug in the overhead cupboard and made a strong coffee that she drank at her desk in the brightly lit open office space shared with twenty others on the ground floor. Her co-workers didn't look up or acknowledge her in any way except for John, who she shared an open cubicle with, and even he barely managed to grunt a good morning. During one of her black periods, she blamed her mother for home schooling her, raising her with no social skills and giving her no friends. Her mother cried for days; it was awful. She'd never make that mistake again.

Being awkward got Tara down. Not knowing how to act with people was a curse, seeming rude when she was being truthful and staying silent while wracking her brain to think of conversation. Today, though, being ignored was a gift because she had no energy for chat.

"Have you got it?"

Tara swivelled her chair to face the tall, slim fashionista looming over her, arms folded. "Have what?"

Joan rolled her eyes behind her red-rimmed designer glasses that perched on her perfect nose, the glasses that matched her red lipstick and her fitted shirt tucked into her tight-waisted black pants. "Oh my God, Tara, the report! The one that was due with me yesterday? Do you have it or do I have to ask someone else to do it?"

Oh no, the report. Tara did have it, but couldn't think where she saved it ... pressure; she was no good under pressure. She switched her PC on, hoping Joan would go away, but she stood waiting while Tara entered her password (Mother123!), praying the location of the file would come to her before the inevitable migraine.

"Tara, can I see you for a minute?" She turned to find Barry standing, almost shoulder to shoulder with Joan. He nodded towards his office. Joan stared at him but didn't budge. "The report, Tara. Have you got it?" she asked.

Worms wriggled in the peripheral of Tara's vision. She looked from Barry to Joan and back to Barry.

"You must come to my office now, Tara," he said and left.

"Sorry, Joan," Tara said. "Better do what he says ... I'll send you the report when I find it."

"This is ridiculous!" Joan turned on her high heels and stomped off towards her office at the end of the room, her black fringed bob unmoving like that actress from *Pulp Fiction*.

Tara followed Barry into his office and closed the door.

She took the seat he offered and he pulled a chair alongside her, resting his elbows on his knees.

"Tara, thanks for coming," he said, his voice much softer than a minute ago. "How are you getting on?"

The change of atmosphere was unexpected. "Uhm. Good, thanks. I'm sorry about the report for Joan, I have it done but couldn't think with her standing over me like that."

"Don't worry. I'll have a word. Joan can be intimidating, but she's a good team leader. Do your job and don't let her fluster you. Is there anything else we can help with to make things more comfortable for you here?"

"Like what?"

He knitted his chubby fingers together. "You've been doing basic roles for a long time now, long before I arrived on the scene. Do you like them?"

Tara shrugged. "I suppose."

"Would you like to try something more challenging? It must get boring." He wheeled backwards in his chair to a grey steel filing cabinet and pulled out a green A4 folder which he handed to her.

Vacancy for Customer Liaison Team Leader, the label read.

"Take this down to the canteen," Barry said. "Read it over some breakfast and let me know what you think. Okay?"

Tara placed the folder on his desk. "No, thanks. I don't want to go to the canteen and I don't want to change my job. I'm fine."

He pushed it back to her. "It wasn't a suggestion. Read it over a cuppa while I deal with Joan. The position closes at midday today, so you don't have long to decide. It could be good for you to push yourself – you're well able for it."

Tara hated the basement canteen. She opened her Tupperware lunchbox and bit into one of Mary's cherry scones while colleagues chatted and laughed at other tables. What was so wrong with her that she couldn't make friends? People took advantage of her, walked on her and inevitably made a fool of her. She was a joke to them. Maybe if she took this promotion, they would respect her. With that thought, her brain fog lifted and she remembered where she'd stored the report. She'd give the figures a final once-over before sending them on, but Joan could wait while she finished her scone. And possibly another cup of coffee.

3

TARA

After a leisurely second cup, and in her own time, Tara emailed the report to Joan, then printed and delivered it to her by hand to make a point. Joan swiped it from her, cursing under her breath.

Taking her time felt like a mini-win, a stand-up for herself, and she was pretty chuffed as Barry approached. He stopped outside his office door.

"Well?" he mouthed to Tara. "The job?" He gave her the thumbs-up and raised his eyebrows.

Tara gave him the thumbs-up back and Barry's face broke into a huge smile. Her phone pinged.

New email from Cassandra Blake.

She thought her legs would give way but managed to make it back to her desk without collapsing, where she opened the email.

Hello Tara,

I am so glad you contacted me, hun, and sorry I'm only getting back to you now.

I see on the MyFamily site that we are full matches and I think by our ages you must be my little sister.

Tara gasped.

"You alright?" John asked, still working away on his keyboard.

"I'm fine." A sister? She kept reading.

I'd love to meet. How's tonight, hun? I can't wait.

TTYL
Cassie

A sister. Her heart leapt and she felt giddy. A million questions flew through her mind, including what TTYL meant, and she needed answers. She hit reply.

Dear Cassie,

Thank you so much for answering my emails. Apologies for sending so many. I promise I'm not a nutter.

She deleted the last line.

I am so excited and would love to meet you. This is a big shock; I've never had a sister or a brother, but I've always wanted one. I can meet any place and time once it's in Dublin after 9 p.m. as I work and then look after Mother.

Looking forward to hearing from you,
Tara Ryan

Tara stared at her phone. She had an older sister, a full sister, which meant she wasn't an only child, and never was. This was thrilling, and she couldn't help but wish she'd known she wasn't alone growing up. She could have really done with another child in her life, but the pennies were dropping too fast to linger on regrets. Because she was concerned too. If Cassie was her older sister, that meant her parents had another child they'd never ever mentioned. Did they have her before they were married? A shiver ran through her, as she thought about that children's home on the news and her mother's reaction to Joan's DNA test. "No good can come from digging up the past," she'd said.

Taken from vulnerable women, often unmarried mothers, the newsreader said, *and sold to the highest bidders,* the woman had added.

Her parents both came from Mayo before settling in Dublin. Did they give Cassandra – Cassie – away and, if so, was it by choice or were they forced to? They were such great parents, Tara couldn't imagine they would give away a child voluntarily, yet why didn't they ever tell her she had a sister?

She couldn't wait to meet Cassie. Mother always said she had two feet but one mouth and she should think about her words before she said them. She considered adding her phone number to the foot of the email, then decided against it, for fear she would come on too strong. She reread her email and clicked send. Her phone beeped almost immediately.

Hi again, hun,

I'm in Mayo but can make it to Dublin this evening no problem, hun. Name the time and place and I'll be there. Here's a pic of me so you'll know who I am, send me a pic of you.

TTYL
Cassie

"Are you sure you're okay?" John asked.

She turned to find him staring.

"Yes, thanks." Tara smiled to reassure him, then turned back to her monitor and opened a spreadsheet, pretending to work, pretending her whole world had not been turned upside down by the phone in her hand. She felt John's eyes on the back of her head, still watching while she entered random data. Only when she heard him tap-tapping his keyboard again did she return to her phone and open the attachment.

The picture.

A woman with brown hair tied back and blue eyes; she was like Tara in a distant way, like a cousin or an aunt. Older but slimmer, and very pretty, but also – and Tara hated to think this way – if she was honest, Cassie looked rough. In fact, she would have crossed the road had they met on the street. She attached her employee ID photo and hurried a reply.

Hi Cassie,

Thank you for the picture. You are very pretty. Here is a picture of me.

Can you meet tonight in Brooke's Bar South Anne Street
at 10 p.m.?

Kind regards,
Tara

Brooke's Bar was the local haunt of her colleagues, and if
it was good enough for Barry's birthday party, it was good
enough for her. Her phone beeped and John sighed. "Can
you please mute that thing? Some of us are trying to work."
The email said:

I'll see you there, hun

Tara settled in to do some work, but the letters and
numbers on her monitor blotted out while wriggly squiggles
formed in her peripheral vision like a moving frame. The
migraine from the fuss earlier, or maybe the day's events,
was coming after all. She searched through the papers in her
desk drawers for her prescription painkillers but the card
was empty. She had to get them and fast, otherwise this
headache would be a three-day event with closed curtains
and darkened rooms. Then she'd be going to meet nobody.
Shutting down her PC to the backdrop of John's complaints,
she went to see Barry.

"Ah, Tara. Take a seat. Delighted that you've put yourself
forward for the management role in customer— What's
wrong?"

Tara stayed standing. "Sorry, I have to take the rest of the
day off. I don't feel well."

He tugged at his blue shirt collar. "I don't know, it's very short notice and the team are under pressure. Did you run it by Joan?"

"No. I have a headache. I have to get medication as soon as possible and lie down or I'll have it for days." Tara's migraine had progressed to her vision. She couldn't make out Barry's features; it was as if a layer of skin had been pulled over his head.

"Okay, I suppose you'd better go. I hope you feel better soon."

Outside the building, the fresh air cooled her cheeks and she felt marginally better, but time was of the essence. Twenty minutes from the time of the swimming vision was her limit to get the medication in and the pharmacy that held her rolling prescription was two streets away. She fetched her sunglasses from her backpack and put them on. If she focused on breathing deeply and didn't look at the low November sun, she could make it. The minute Tara said the words migraine, the pharmacist sat her down, rushed into the back room and returned with two pills and a soft plastic cup of water.

There Tara sat, eyes closed and in silence until she felt the first ease of the headache. Doctor Lucas had warned the headaches would worsen with age and he was right. "Hormonal," he said. More suffering from useless female hormones that she never wanted and never used.

Within the hour, Tara felt better. In fact, she felt perfect. Buoyed by the codeine in the pills, Tara headed back to the office and her thoughts returned to her date later that evening with her sister. *Her sister.* She couldn't show up to meet the woman who shared her DNA looking like this, could she? The right thing was to go back to work, but she continued past the building and towards the city. Time to go shopping – her least favourite activity in the world. Fifteen minutes later she reached Grafton Street and started with Primmies for the Modern Lady, where she shopped for her mother's clothes.

"A stunning dress, darling," the glamorous assistant said in the fitting room as she passed the black and port midi dress through the curtains to Tara, the same dress as the one on the mannequin outside. "Winter florals are very popular with women our age, but you might need a different size."

Tara accepted the dress through the gap in the curtain. "No, I don't need a different size. That's my size and we're not the same age. You're much older than me."

The dress fit and Tara brought it to the till. The assistant, now much cooler, wrapped it in tissue paper and put it into a white paper bag with a handle made of black ribbon. "That will be €370.50. Cash or card?"

Tara waited.

"Is there something else?" the shop assistant asked.

"Yes. I'd like the rest too, please."

The woman's eyes widened. "Excuse me?"

Tara pointed to the mannequin. "I said I want what she's wearing. I mean all of it. I take a seven in shoes."

The assistant lit up and danced her way around the shop, returning with a leather jacket, velvet ankle boots and cross-over handbag, all in black. She boxed the gold-plated necklace and bracelet from the display cabinet and popped in a complementary scarf. One ecstatic shop assistant and four white bags later, Tara left, feeling like Julia Roberts in *Pretty Woman*.

It was still only 2 p.m. Tara chanced the fancy hair salon next door to see if they had a free spot. The Christmas season was well underway and it was unlikely they would, but when she walked in with all her bags, a stylist brought her straight to a chair and asked what she could do for her. When she said the stylist could do whatever the stylist liked, the young, very beautiful woman clapped her hands and squealed with delight. A shoulder-length bob with a chocolate base and highlights later, Tara was fabulous, according to the hairdresser, as she relieved her credit card of another €280. She didn't mind. Having no mortgage, no rent and few grocery bills left her with a bank account so healthy she never checked her balance. She probably had thousands – no, tens of thousands – of euros in there.

Back on Grafton Street, considering what to eat for lunch, Tara's phone rang with a 6079 number – Partners Plus – which she promptly declined. This was her personal phone not her work phone; they shouldn't be calling her, that was the rule. Mother said work belonged in work and not to let them take advantage and, for that reason, her work phone was at home in a drawer somewhere. If she didn't carry it, she couldn't be contacted. There were two other missed calls from the same number she hadn't heard, but the hair salon was noisy with hairdryers and pop music blaring. She thought of returning the call for a moment before muting her phone. Whatever it was could wait until tomorrow.

Her last stop was the pharmacy beside Pearse Street station with the flaking white exterior that advertised free makeovers. The heavily made-up woman with the red eyes and tobacco breath told her all about the products and how much they cost as she applied them, but Tara wasn't at all interested. The woman didn't look happy when Tara left thirty minutes later with none of the products she'd spoken about and one arm as long as the other.

The journey home on the train was a very different experience than the vomit comet of that morning, a head at medicated ease and a tummy full of excited butterflies. In four hours, she was going to meet her sister for the first time. A sister that she didn't know existed this time yesterday. A sister – the one thing she'd always wished for.

She called a cab and booked it for later, wondering who the glamorous woman reflected in the carriage window was before copping it was herself. She looked different, which Mary proved for sure when she came in her front door.

"Tara, is that really you? Your hair ... your make-up ... you look different!" Then her eyes twinkled. "Are you going somewhere nice?"

Tara hung her coat up and went into the living room. Mary followed.

"No, Mother. I'm going to meet—" She stopped. She couldn't tell her; not yet, anyway. No surprises and no upsets, Doctor Lucas said, and this was a surprise of epic proportions. It would probably kill her stone dead.

"Tara ..." Mary's voice was croaky. "Who are you going to meet?"

"A colleague – at 10 p.m. in town."

Mary smiled. "Is it a gentleman colleague?"

"No, Mother. God! It's a female colleague."

"Ah, I know it is, I'm pulling your leg. Is it that Joan you were telling me about? I'm very happy for you, but be careful. You're very impressionable, shocking easy led. Anyone could take you for a mug."

I'm not as stupid as you think, Mother ... is what Tara wanted to say.

"Yes, Mother. I'll be careful," is what she actually said, then demolished the chicken curry, naan breads and rice.

Mary watched her eat. "It's very late to be going out. Why didn't you cancel dinner with me? I wouldn't have minded. I don't want to be a burden on you."

Tara dabbed her mouth with her napkin. Mary always trotted out the not-a-burden line when she got a feeling something was going on in Tara's life, which was rare. It was all lies – she always, *always* minded when Tara didn't make it over for dinner.

"No, Mother. I said I'd be here and I'm here. You're no burden."

Mary reached across the table and placed her ice-cold hand, its blue veins snaking through her sharp bones, on Tara's.

Tara didn't stay for the cup of tea, tucking Mary into bed earlier than usual and switching on the main evening news on the TV in her room.

"You get off now," Mary said, stroking a purring Snowy. "Don't worry about putting me to bed so early. I'll be fine, although it is very early and I'm wide awake." Her lined face told a different story. She was tired and would be asleep in minutes.

In the bathroom, Tara changed into her new clothes. This room was a godsend. After the accident, Mary couldn't even manage the toilet. She'd gotten years of use out of it before needing the bag last year.

She checked herself in the hall mirror. She looked so different. Good different. She peeped in to say goodnight to Mary, but she was fast asleep as expected, with the TV still on. Tara took the remote control from her mother's hand to switch it off when the reporter caught her attention.

Continuing with the scandal currently rocking the country, we spoke to Linda Hynes and Maura Geraghty about their story in the Cherish the Child home.

A red-haired woman around Tara's age and a white-haired, older woman sat at a kitchen table with two mugs in front of them. The older woman spoke.

"Linda, or Debbie, as I named her, was taken from me at birth. I was nursing in County General and was in a relationship with a doctor from England. He was lovely to me, we were besotted with each other and planned to get engaged. Then I fell pregnant and everything changed. He went back to his wife and three children he had failed to mention in our six-month relationship and my parents tortured me until I agreed to give up the baby."

The older lady stopped to take a breath and the younger one squeezed her hand.

"Maura, my birth mother, spent her whole life looking for me, despite being told to forget me 'for my own good'. Every door she knocked on was slammed in her face. I was sold for £4,000 on condition my adoptive parents signed a nondisclosure agreement; a gagging order, promising never to tell me."

"Did you ever suspect anything?" the reporter asked and the red-haired woman sighed. *"No, never. My parents were good people but they never told me; I suppose they were afraid of the consequences if they did."*

"They were told they could go to prison if they opened their mouths," the old lady cut in. *"They are victims in this hell as much as we are. We all suffered – all of us."*

A car beeped from outside but if it was the taxi, it could wait. Tara was engrossed in the TV.

"May I ask how you found each other?" the reporter asked the daughter.

"Last year, my adopted mother died of a long illness. She left

*me a letter telling me everything – how she had been sworn to
secrecy and lived in fear of me being taken from her, but on her
death bed she wanted to do the right thing. I'm so glad she did."*
"There wasn't a day in my life I didn't look for Debbie – I
mean Linda. Not a day. I never married or had children, how
could I? I was destroyed, and I wasn't the only one. *They pulled
our babies from our arms to sell to the highest bidder and told us
they were gone to the best homes, to good Catholic married
parents. It was human trafficking, gaslighting, and someone has
to pay.*"

The taxi beeped from outside again. Tara switched off
the telly and kissed her mother on her protruding cheek-
bone. She was so vulnerable, lying there. Was Cassandra
taken from her and she sworn to secrecy? Did Daddy know
he had another daughter, or did she go away to a mother
and baby home and come back with no baby and never
tell?

Fifteen minutes early, Tara arrived in Brooke's Bar. It was
almost empty, a few lone drinkers at the bar looking up from
their pints, but there was no sign of anyone who resembled
Cassie.

"What can I do you for?" the bearded barman asked.
"Something to settle the nerves?"

Tara hid her trembling hands. "Um, I don't know. I
suppose something with alcohol."

He looked at the top shelf. "What's your poison?"

She shrugged. "I don't know. What would you
recommend?"

His eyes sparkled. "How about a cocktail?"

She furrowed her brow. "I don't know, they're very strong,
aren't they?"

"I'll tell you what. I'll make you my signature cocktail,

The Charmer, and if you don't like it, you can try something else, free of charge. How does that sound?"

Tara smiled. "Sounds fair."

A man sitting at the bar rolled up his newspaper and left. Tara took his place on his high stool, still warm, and checked her phone. No messages.

"Ta dah!" The barman put a long brown drink with ice and lemon on the bar in front of Tara. She took a sip.

"Well?"

"Delicious!" It was delicious, like the most refreshing cola ice pop ever. It went down easy, so easy she polished it off, paid and ordered another one.

"What's your usual tipple?" the barman asked, shaking the cocktail maker.

Tara found it surprisingly easy to talk to him and he was quite handsome, which helped. "A glass of wine."

"A good choice, madam."

She chuckled and checked her phone again. 22:07. No messages. Cassie was late but not very late. The second cocktail was even nicer than the first, if that was possible. Tara watched her phone and, with no sign of Cassie, she ordered another drink. By 11 p.m., she was well tipsy and had to accept Cassie wasn't coming. She sighed, so disappointed and hurt to be stood up by her unknown sister. She finished her drink and put her new leather jacket on, ready to go home.

"Thank you so much and goodnight," she said to the barman.

He glanced up from his newspaper, then something caught his eye. "Hold on a minute, there seems to be a bit of trouble outside."

Tara wobbled. "What sort of trouble?"

"Ah, we get a lot of down and outs around here since the homeless place opened on the next street. Never needed security until then; now we can't keep the staff. Do-gooders, you know, bleeding-hearts, but they won't have them on their own doorsteps. Scum is scum, no matter how you dress it up."

Tara tried to process the mean words he spewed after being such a nice man all night when a woman screamed outside. "Get your fucking hands off me. That's assault!"

Tara stood up onto the rung of the high stool and peered out the window, over the red velvet half-curtain hanging from the fake gold bar. A burly security guard manhandled a dark-haired woman who flailed and punched while a crowd gathered around them.

He flung her to the ground, holding his face. "That's assault, you animal. I said you're not getting in, now sling your hook!" A line of blood trailed down his cheek. She clambered to her feet before falling back onto the ground.

"Enjoying the show?" she screamed at the crowd before glancing at the window of the pub and catching Tara's eye.

It was Cassie.

4

CASSIE

Tuesday, 8 November

Cassie Blake hated the 10:30 p.m. curfew at Dignity House, but tonight it couldn't come quick enough. She lay on the grey flannelette duvet of her single bed, braiding her long brown hair, her blue eyes fixed on the mahogany wardrobe in the far corner like a cat stalking a bird. Most nights she'd be found trying to blag her way out for one last smoke, but not tonight.

Any minute Sharon would come to tuck her in. Before 11 p.m., the night counsellor on duty called to each bedroom to say goodnight and check up on the women and children who stayed there. Dignity House was an alcohol- and drug-free zone; being found with any banned substance in this refuge meant immediate expulsion, and she was not risking that.

It was a rare lucky moment for Cassie when she woke up

to find Sharon in her ward in County General Hospital. Despite Cassie's reputation, her past and continuing problems, Sharon took pity on her and offered her a room at the inn. Cassie swore, like she had many times before, that she wouldn't mess up the opportunity, but this time she was determined to keep her word. It felt like her last chance.

The staff in Dignity House were kind but firm and, as long as the residents caused no trouble and played by the rules, they had no issue – the staff had a pleasant working environment and the residents got a safe place to call home for as long as they needed it. In the thirteen weeks and three days Cassie was there, the few residents that had moved out were kicked out. Homeless, unemployed and unemployable, that summed her up, but she wasn't alone; there were many women there like her, some with a rake of kids. Not that they were friends. Cassie kept herself to herself. She'd been in the game long enough to know to be friendly but not befriend, to trust but not get close. Letting others in only ever ended in getting burned and Cassie had enough hurt to last her a lifetime. Besides, they may have been in the same situation but there were no besties in this dog-eat-dog underworld. A world where you could lose your teeth over a simple misunderstanding.

It wasn't that she was scared – Cassie was no coward and had been well able to look out for herself since childhood – but it was nice, for once, not having to.

Self-preservation from necessity, Sharon called it.

The refuge was a three-storey period house covered in ivy and well hidden from the main road behind evergreen trees. The view was spectacular: rolling green fields leading to the beach, and mountains rising in the distance across the bay. The refuge was on the outskirts of the surfing town of Lenburgh, geographically not too far from where she grew up and yet a million miles away in every other way. Donated by the local celebrity and reformed alcoholic Maurice Cleary, there were eight en-suite bedrooms, a shared kitchen, a TV room and a conservatory to the back for reading and taking time out. An office with a heavy door marked PRIVATE was to the right of the front door. This was for staff and daily counselling sessions, although they were more likely to happen casually over a cup of tea than behind a closed door. Cassie had stayed in places where closing her eyes at night was a risk, but here, by the wild Atlantic Ocean, she felt safe and slept like a baby, her nightmares having all but stopped. It wasn't a Hallmark movie; she had a lot of stuff she still needed to work through. But this was the calmest she'd felt in years. Until this afternoon. But that was not her fault.

Room 6 was Cassie's room. Bright but sparse, with lemon walls and an old oak floor that she cleaned and polished daily. It was small but had everything she needed. A single bed was pushed into the corner with a single pine nightstand to its left, where, right now a two-litre bottle of cola and a pack of Marlboros sat along with that dreadful letter. An enlarged print of butterflies in pinks, yellows and purples on the wall was reflected in the full-length mirror opposite her bed, with an inspirational quote that, for a while, Cassie actually believed.

"There is always hope."

Cassie lay deadly still watching the wardrobe.

There is always hope – such lies. Cassie's life should have been different, she shouldn't have been here in this place with nothing to call her own, but, no matter how hard she tried, it was always one step forward, two steps back. People saw what they wanted to see; she never stood a chance. It was a miracle, though, that she'd got into this place. Here, they gave her hope, something she hadn't had in a very long time, and then took it away again. It wasn't the first time this had happened, but it was the latest and she hated them for it.

Earlier, when Sharon called Cassie into the office and told her to close the door behind her, she should have known it was bad news. The old Cassie would have been ready to put the wall up, been ready for another slap in the face, but this Cassie was softened, this Cassie was a fool. This Cassie had let her guard down.

Sharon invited her to take a seat at her messy desk, covered in papers. "How are you keeping, Cassie?" she asked in her Donegal lilt.

"I'm good, thank you, and you?"

Sharon tilted her head and looked over her glasses at Cassie with pity. Then the penny dropped, from a height.

"I didn't get the job, did I?"

Sharon sighed. "I'm sorry. No, you didn't get it."

With Sharon's encouragement, Cassie had applied for the position of kitchen porter in a small, local seafood restaurant. Sixteen hours a week at first, to see how she got on. Sharon wrote a glowing reference and drove her to the interview in her yellow Mini Cooper, not the Dignity House minibus. In the car park at the back of the restaurant, Sharon released her seatbelt and turned to face her.

"Cassie, you're a great worker, diligent, punctual and industrious. Believe in yourself."

"But what if they've heard ..."

"They've heard nothing about you except that you are a

resident. I told them your reason for being with us is strictly confidential. Now, go get that job!"

Like a fool, Cassie had listened and now her stomach turned with the look in Sharon's eyes. She could handle anything but pity.

"Did they say why I didn't get it?" Cassie asked.

Sharon fixed her glasses and looked up, a tear in her eye. "I'm so sorry, Cassie. They went with another candidate. Please don't let this set you back; you've come so far and you can apply for more jobs, I'll help you."

Cassie laughed. "We both know why they didn't give me the job. It's always going to be the same. If I stay here, I'll have nothing and nobody and never will, and yet I have no way of getting out. I'm penniless and trapped. It's all pointless."

"It's never pointless, Cassie. Never. You have so much to give." Sharon opened a drawer in her desk and took the petty cash box out, placing it on top of the papers. Unlocking it, she handed Cassie a €20 note. "You've earned it, your work is incredible. Maybe we could get you on the rota here."

From the day Cassie moved in, she'd pulled her weight – ironing, washing, polishing, cleaning, cooking, there was so much to do and nothing she wouldn't do, always to the highest standard. Sitting still was not for her, too much time to think, too many shoulda-woulda-couldas to juggle. She'd work until she fell down, yet couldn't get a job in the outside world, this being her fifth rejection in as many days.

She took the money.

"I am so sorry." Sharon apologised again.

A lump formed in Cassie's throat and she jumped up from her chair before Sharon could see her cry. "It doesn't matter. It's fine. I'm fine."

"Cassie, I'm worried about—"

"I said I'm fine. I'll take a walk, clear my head."

"Good idea. Get some sunlight and connect with nature."

Cassie pulled up the hood of her black padded coat and left the grounds of Dignity House on foot. She waved without looking back, the tears streaming down her face.

It was spitting rain and late afternoon, the daylight fading, when she reached the beach. The navy waves of the wild Atlantic Ocean crashed and ebbed, fuller and louder than usual. A storm was on its way for sure.

She popped in her new ear pods and selected a playlist on her phone, both items donated to the refuge by the local branch of a well-known electrical store. Preparing to get lost in her music, she took into a brisk walk, but when, after a few hundred metres, she was still in silence, she stopped and checked her phone.

Unable to connect. Go online to see recommended songs.

No internet connection available.

Damn it. No phone credit, which meant no data, which meant no bloody music.

The lights of Lenburgh twinkled in the distance against the darkening sky. The €20 Sharon gave her would buy phone credit for the month and the shops were half an hour's walk away, tops. She pulled her hood tighter around her face and headed towards the town.

It was fully dark when Cassie reached O'Reilly's, the compact illuminated supermarket on the main street of Lenburgh, and the rain was bucketing down. Dripping, she queued for the one open checkout, smiling at the elderly customer hunched over her shopping basket ahead. The old lady bent down and put the items up onto the belt, one by one. Did she live alone? She must have been at least eighty years old. It hit Cassie in the face like a sledgehammer. She wasn't looking at herself years from now; it was much worse than that. She'd be alone and homeless. Holding onto the end of the conveyor belt, she closed her eyes and focused on her breathing. In for four, out for six. Thinking ahead was pointless ... no point in meeting trouble halfway ... one day at a time.

Perspective – a few months ago, it didn't look like she'd even make it until today, never mind grow old. The old lady looked up from her shopping basket and smiled at her.

"Do you need a hand?" Cassie asked.

"Thank you, young lady, but I think I'll manage," she replied, and Cassie smiled back. Young lady – it had been a while since she'd been called that.

She should be grateful, though; she had a safe place to lie and was almost fourteen weeks sober. Practise an attitude of gratitude for the small things, like they said, help out when she could.

Clink. Clink.

The familiar sound of bottles knocking together sent a shiver through her. It came from the softly lit area behind the salon doors to her left. She knew exactly what was beyond there.

Distraction.

Cassie planned her evening. Return to the refuge, watch some TV and have a chat with Sharon, be honest about her feelings. She'd get through this setback, she had to.

Clink, Clink.

Affirmation.

Cassie closed her eyes and repeated in her mind, "*You are brave, you are strong, you are a miracle.*"

Clink. Clink. Clink.

Higher power –Nothing here.

Cassie had nobody and believed in nobody's god.

Bing bong. "Hello shoppers," a woman announced over the tannoy. "Tuesday is Choose Day in O'Reilly's Value Store. Check out our special deals. Twelve pack of toilet rolls €3.49, four bread rolls for one euro and in our off-licence—"

Oh, no.

"Golshoff Vodka, 1 litre bottle ..."

La, la, la, la, la.

"Was €45 now €30."

Cassie didn't remember much after that, except insisting she help the old dear and helping herself to money from her purse.

It was 10:45 p.m. when Sharon came in and sat on the edge of her bed. "Are you alright?"

Cassie diverted her gaze away from the wardrobe. "Not really, but I will be. It's tough but I'm tougher."

"That's it. Hang in there. Something will turn up, I know it. Get some rest and I'll see you in the morning for breakfast duty. 6 a.m. You're making the porridge, okay?"

"Porridge it is." Cassie snuggled under the duvet and faced the wall. "Goodnight, Sharon, and thank you. You've been so good to me, I'm so grateful, but right now I want to be alone."

"Of course." Sharon switched off the light as she left the room. Cassie listened intently as Sharon checked in on the other residents before returning to her office and closing the door, then she tiptoed over to the wardrobe and removed the black holdall from inside the door.

Over three months since she'd had a drink. *Thirteen weeks and five days.* She released the bottle of vodka from the bag and unscrewed the top, a sound sweeter than any symphony. A sound that whispered, *Welcome home.*

She lifted the heavy bottle and put it to her mouth, letting the liquid pour in. How malicious was it, putting the alcohol beside the one working checkout in the only supermarket in town and then announcing it for all to hear? They knew exactly what they were doing; she couldn't be the only one struggling. Taking advantage of the vulnerable, this was all their fault.

She could have got the phone credit in the post office, but she wasn't going near Mrs O'Leary, the old weapon who ran it. Such a poisonous old biddy, spreading gossip from behind the counter. Cassie couldn't help but wonder if she had anything to do with her not getting the job. Not that it mattered anymore anyway. Nothing did.

The vodka burned then soothed her throat, each drop releasing a million tensions and memories, blocking the pain. She took a breath.

"Ah, it's good to be back," she said, before returning the bottle to her lips and glugging the remainder of its contents.

5

CASSIE

Wednesday, 9 November

The midday sun beat down on her, making her scalp sweat and her arms itch. She was back there again; back in the cornfields. She cradled her bare feet to stretch out her aching back and counted the flowers on her faded blue dress. She'd been here a while, hunched in the same spot, terrified to move even an inch. Mammy said when They, the people in suits, came to run and hide and not to come out until they left. One of them, a woman, was in the house now. She plucked a dandelion from the ground and blew the seeds, wishing the woman would leave. She plucked another and then another, dropping it when she heard footsteps approach. Run, she should run, but she was paralysed. Cassie tried to scream but nothing came. Trapped in her own body, the leaves of the corn plants reached out and wrapped around her ankles. She could see the woman's shoes now. High brown shoes with wooden heels and *laces. With all her might she inhaled, filled her lungs with air and screamed. And screamed and screamed and ...*

"Cassie. Wake up, wake up!" Someone was shaking her. "Wake up, Cassie!"

She gasped for breath.

"It's a dream. Just a dream." That lulling Donegal accent.

Cassie tried to open her eyes, but they were glued shut. Her head throbbed and her stomach burned. She hadn't had that dream since moving to Dignity House, but this time it felt more real than ever before.

"Can you pass me the Coke from my nightstand, Sharon?" she asked.

Wait, why is Sharon in my room?

A warm hand touched her hand. "Oh, Cassie."

She forced her eyes open, the pain in her head intensifying, to the glare of a bright hospital ward and Sharon's pitiful eyes.

"Where am I?" she tried to say, but the words caught like vomit in her raw throat. She gagged and Sharon shoved a plastic bowl under her chin just in time.

"That's it. Good girl, get it all up," she said, rubbing Cassie's back.

"Where am I?" Cassie asked again.

"County General. You were brought here in an ambulance in the early hours of this morning."

Cassie's world shattered as she remembered the vodka. "Oh."

Sharon's eyes widened. "Oh? Is that all you have to say? Oh??? Cassie! You were doing so well. Thirteen weeks and five days sober. Would have been fourteen weeks tomorrow."

She tried to think quickly. Denial was her usual first defence when she fell off the wagon but, as she was lying in hospital, it would appear she was well past that point. After denial, unconditional apologies coupled with promises led to the best outcome. "I won't do it again; I promise if you—"

Sharon diverted her gaze to the trolley at the foot of the bed where the black holdall sat beside a plastic jug of water and a glass. "I'm sorry, Cassie. You've been evicted from the refuge."

Evicted? No, she couldn't leave. "Please, don't do this, Sharon. Dignity House is the best thing that ever happened to me. It wasn't my fault, I can explain."

Sharon diverted her gaze. It was time to take it up a notch. Tears, and lots of them. "I'm so, so sorry. Please, Sharon, don't make me go. I have nowhere to go and no one. Please! It was a slip. I can do better."

Sharon joined her hands as if in prayer. "Cassie, I'm sorry too, I truly am, but you can't come back. There are vulnerable women and children there and, Mother of God, but you almost died, Cassie. This wasn't a slip; you planned this. You bought the alcohol, brought it back, hid it and planned to drink it. You had many opportunities to come talk to me, you knew the deal when you came to stay – no alcohol or illegal substances under any circumstances, and you chose to break them. I'm sorry, but your time with us has passed and you have to go."

Cassie was in full flow now, sobbing with tears streaming down her cheeks. "I'm so sorry but it wasn't my fault. I was in the supermarket and there was a special offer on the vodka—"

"Stop it! For God's sake, Cassie, stop it! Yes, you've had a hard life, harder than most, and yes, what happened to you wasn't fair, but you're an adult with adult responsibilities. You can blame the world for your problems forever but, at some point, you have to grow up and be accountable for your own actions. Sorry, Cassie, I have tried to help you, I gave you a chance that people would give their right arm for and you threw it away. Nobody forced that vodka down your throat. You knew the rules, this was your fault and your time in Dignity House has come to an end." Sharon turned on her heels. "Sort yourself out before it's too late," she said, not looking back, and then she left.

Cassie turned away and cried. Real tears this time. She was such a screw up, everything she touched turned to shit. But then she got angry. This wasn't about the drinking. Not really. This was about people always waiting for her to fail. She never stood a chance, despite what they claimed. The story of Cassie's life. She was a fool to believe their false claims of care and fondness, she'd let her guard down, but she wouldn't let it happen again. No, Cassie managed better in this world with just herself to look after and herself to let down. From here on in, she was going to look out for number one. She closed her eyes.

"One, two, three – lift."

A whisper of nurses in soft shoes woke her as they transferred an old lady from a trolley and set up the medical equipment she was attached to.

A full brown perm lay on the white pillow with a tiny face under it, yellow like the flowers on the curtain they pulled around her bed, which now obscured Cassie's view.

A pretty blonde nurse in pink scrubs backed out from the split in the curtains. "Now, Brigid, you'll be fine here for the moment. We're getting your ward ready for you." She glanced over at Cassie.

"Ah, Cassandra, I heard you were back with us. You gave us some fright. How are you feeling?"

She knew her name. "Rough. My throat is like sandpaper, but I'll live. You can't kill a bad thing."

The nurse folded her arms and pursed her lips. "You nearly *didn't* live, chicken. Who knows what would have happened if you weren't found when you were. You'd stopped breathing, did you know that?"

"I didn't."

The nurse pointed to the ceiling. "Someone up there was looking out for you – again!"

A higher power? Rubbish.

"Can I get you something to eat? Some tea and toast?"

That's exactly what Cassie needed. "Yes, that would be great, thank you. Can you pass my bag, please?"

The nurse gave her the heavy backpack before taking her leave to fetch the food. Cassie zipped it open to find her clothes, neatly packed with her phone and charger on top. She tumbled all her worldly goods, as donated by others, onto the bed. Three pairs of leggings, one pair of jeans, two jumpers, three tops, three pairs of sports socks, two bras and three packs of unopened knickers. Her washbag was packed with all her toiletries and her make-up bag was tucked down the end beside her hairbrush. All clean.

Being clean improved her chances of getting a decent bed for the night, or being accepted into a Bed and Breakfast, if she managed to get a voucher from social welfare. She'd have to find a hostel before they kicked her out of here. She dialled the first number in her contacts: Avondale Lodge. The owner was a snotty bitch, and there was a high chance of it being fully booked for the night at this stage, but it was the nicest place that took in her likes. The dregs.

You do not have sufficient funds to place this call.

"Fuuuuuuu—!"

"Keep your voice down!" The nurse was back. "And watch your mouth; we've older people in here who don't want to hear that language."

"Sorry. I've no credit to ring a hostel and I've nowhere to go and no money. I'm screwed."

The nurse glanced at the door and reached into the pocket of her trousers. "If you're super quick you can use my hotspot. Will that help?"

Cassie jumped at the chance and connected. Before she could make a call, an email notification popped up at the top of her screen. Then another. And another! Scanning through them quickly, she couldn't believe her eyes.

Emails from a woman called Tara Ryan.

6

TARA

Wednesday, 9 November

Tara rushed to the entrance of the pub. "Let me out, please," she begged the tall, broad security guard blocking the doorway.

He looked Tara up and down, the blood forming a red trail down his cheek. It looked like a deep gash that would need stitches. "A couple more minutes, there, love. Waiting for the trash to take itself out."

"I need to leave. The woman on the ground is my ... my ... I know her."

He whistled and stood aside. "If I were you, I'd take her far away from here before she gets herself killed."

Tara rushed to Cassie and helped her to her feet, the smell of cigarettes nearly knocking her out. She wore a wine hoody and black jeans, both filthy. Her runners were white underneath the black dirt and a black padded coat was in a heap on the ground beside her.

"And don't come back," the security guard called after them as they left. Cassie swung around and gave him the middle finger, much to Tara's mortification. She linked Cassie down the cobblestones of South William Street and on towards Grafton Street.

"I need ... I need to sit down," Cassie said, and Tara found a vacant metal bench outside the hairdressers she'd visited only hours ago.

"Thank you, hun."

"Tara. My name is Tara."

Cassie didn't answer. Her eyes were half-closed and her brown hair was matted.

"Cassie, I'm Tara. You came to Dublin to meet me. The DNA test, remember?"

A confused look turned to a smile. "Ah, yes, of course. Tara!" She broke into a laugh that was silent apart from the rattling in her chest. "I'm Cassie, the successful, good-looking sister." She stopped abruptly and examined Tara's face. "You're gorgeous."

"No, I'm not. I'm not gorgeous."

Cassie touched her face then, leaning against her, closed her eyes. Together they sat in silence, Cassie not moving and Tara wishing she would. When the snoring started, and a gang of youths pushed against her, Tara had had enough. She shook Cassie by the shoulder. "Hey, wake up. I have to go home."

"Can I stay with you tonight?" she slurred, her eyes still closed.

"I'm sorry, but you can't. It wouldn't be safe. I don't know anything about you and you're obviously drunk. Mother always said—"

Cassie opened her eyes. "Don't you dare look down your nose at me. You don't know anything about me."

"I'm ... I'm not looking down my nose at you. We can meet tomorrow night again. I have to work tomorrow but afterwards. Do you have to get back to Mayo to work?"

Cassie laughed again. "Work? Ha. I don't even have a place to sleep tonight, where would I work? I thought my long-lost sister would put me up. Give me money for a hostel at least."

Money for a hostel, Tara knew what that meant. She'd heard it a million times walking past the addiction centre on the way from work to the train. On her first day in the job, Human Resources warned not to give money to the addicts who gathered there; they would claim it was for a hostel but would use it for drugs or alcohol.

"I'm sorry, I can't." Tara stood to leave.

Cassie grabbed her wrist. "You owe me. You're my sister. You think you're better than me in your fancy clothes but we're the same inside." She put her other hand on Tara's heart and stared into her eyes. "In here."

Tara yanked her hand away. "No, we're not. I was excited to meet you, but you showed up like this. I got my hair done and my makeup and even bought a new outfit and you're a filthy mess. We are not the same. No way, Jose, no way."

She shrugged Cassie off and ran all the way down Grafton Street, afraid to stop in case Cassie followed. Only when she got to the end of the street did she look back. Cassie was gone.

Tara was close to tears by the time she reached Pearse Street train station. The monitor showed a train due in three minutes and she searched her new handbag for her wallet, rifling through its many pockets and zips.

"Are you okay?" the man checking the tickets asked as she tumbled out her belongings onto the ground.

Tara's head swam. "My wallet. It must be in here somewhere. I had it when I left home this morning and I used it tonight. My train ticket is in it."

He opened the gate. "Go on through," he said. "I know your face well. Hope someone didn't steal it on you."

7

TARA

Thursday, 10 November

Tara awoke long before her alarm with her makeup still on and her clothes from the night before strewn on her bedroom floor. Two more days until Saturday, when she'd clean it all up, not that it mattered.

She lay in the disappointment. In one day, she'd discovered she had a sister and that sister was a drunk. "Be careful what you wish for," Mother said whenever Tara begged for a sibling as a child. "We love you to the moon and back. You have no idea how lucky you are."

She dragged herself to the bathroom and turned on the shower, but the effort was too much and she decided against it, putting on a fresh outfit of leggings, skirt and top instead. Her head was fried.

Where did Cassie go after Tara left her in the city centre? Did she get a place to stay after all? What did she do? Maybe she should have let Cassie stay with her. Of course, she should have, what was she thinking? The woman had come all the way from Mayo to meet her at the drop of a hat; it was the least she could have done. She may have been drunk but she was her sister, for God's sake. A thought terrified her. What if Cassie was dead?

She was about to call the police when she remembered. Her wallet was gone. She didn't want to jump to conclusions, but she knew what they'd say and she couldn't forget her own first impression on seeing Cassie's photo.

She'd had a few too many drinks herself; there was every chance she left her wallet in the bar. No need to stereotype people; she hated it when people did that to her, so she was not going to do it back. She fetched her bank card from the book in the filing cabinet. Her mother always said to hide your bank cards in case of burglars and carry a minimum amount of cash in case of pickpockets. A few euros, her work ID, and a train ticket were all that was gone and the train ticket could be replaced. Outside, the sun shone as Tara took the short walk up the hill by the old houses, around by the church and into the train station. Another day, another dollar.

An unfamiliar ticket attendant manned the turnstiles and insisted Tara join the long queue at the ticket desk to buy a one-day ticket. She'd cancel her annual ticket and order another when she got to work. The queue moved slowly and Tara watched her train come and go on the monitor above her head. Ten minutes later, she joined different faces than usual on the same packed platform.

A down and out made his way along the commuters, begging for money as the train pulled into the station. Most diverted their gaze. Was Cassie's world like this?

The doors of the train carriage opened right in front of Tara and she spied a seat. With laser focus she made for it, getting her bum on the green tartan fabric split seconds before her female rival, who huffed and stood with her backside in Tara's face.

"Morning, Tara. We must stop meeting like this. Like the hair!" Barry was sitting in the seat facing her. "I hope you're feeling better."

Tara touched her hair. She'd forgotten about it. "Thanks, I got it done yesterday after my headache cleared."

"It's nice. Very Rachel from *Friends*."

"Thank you." She looked out the window to hide her heating cheeks, but he kept on talking. He was so weird.

"I'm glad you decided to go for the customer service job. It'll be good for you."

The job – she'd forgotten about the job and the extra responsibility felt too heavy today, an extra hassle she didn't need. "I don't think I'll go for it after all," she said. "I'm grand where I am in data entry. I'm not cut out for customer service."

He gasped, putting his hand to his mouth dramatically. "Oh, Tara, don't say that! You're well able. There's full training and an increase in pay. There's a couple of candidates going for it, but if you want it, it's yours." He leaned closer. "I pulled some strings for you."

He was being so nice, Tara supposed she should be nice back. "Fine, I'll think about it. Did you fix your car?"

He laughed. "No, I'm afraid the car is in palliative care but I'm staying positive and using it as an excuse, I mean reason, to go shopping for a new one. Going to check out new ones this weekend. What would you recommend?"

"I don't know anything about cars, sorry. I don't drive, remember?"

He bit his lip. "I don't suppose you would want to ...? Ah, never mind. Sure, the party is on Saturday night. Have you changed your mind about joining us?"

Tara shook her head.

"Not even for one little—"

"No means no," Tara said.

Barry turned to look out the window, the red creeping up his neck and past his jawline again. They rode the rest of the journey in silence, which suited Tara because she had important things to think about. Over and over, she turned yesterday's events in her head, trying to make sense of it all. As the train pulled into the station, she sent a quick message.

Cassie,

It's Tara. I hope you are okay. I'm sorry you can't stay with me, but I hope you found somewhere to sleep last night.

Please let me know that you are okay, I'm worried about you.

Tara

8

CASSIE

A chink of light streamed through the brocade cream curtains and landed on her mud-stained coat draped over an emerald velvet chair. Cassie lay in the king-size bed of the hotel, the cotton sheets soft, with no idea how she got there.

She met her sister last night, she vaguely remembered that, although if someone told her it was a dream, she'd believe them.

Telling the difference between dreams and reality was always difficult for Cassie and, speaking of dreams, she'd had it again last night. Twice in two days. That was bad.

This dream had been with her since childhood. In it, she was small, hiding from a woman in a field of corn and dandelions. She'd freeze as the woman came for her. When she was little, this dream felt real and she tried to tell anyone who would listen, but they laughed at her, calling her delusional, an attention seeker and a liar. Once upon a time she was sure this was an experience before it became a dream.

Whatever happened last night was not her fault. She

hadn't meant to get drunk, but the unconscious old dear in the hospital brought her purse with her and left it on display. Who does that? The nurses knew why Cassie was in there; they should have known to take away temptation. Still though, she hadn't intended to drink; it was just to get enough to get her to Dublin and pay for a hostel for the night.

She'd caught an afternoon train to Dublin. From Connolly station, she'd walked up Talbot Street towards O'Connell Street, the Christmas lights already switched on, even though it wasn't yet December. Christmas, the most disappointing time of the year ... She hated it. She passed an off-licence, its window a myriad of glistening bottles, and doubled back. It was like Aladdin's cave – bottles of every colour and size, with every drink you could think of and a thinning string of gold tinsel taped around the dirty window. Like a moth to a flame, a child to a sweet shop, an alcoholic to an off-licence, she was powerless to resist. It wasn't her fault.

More light filtered into the hotel room to reveal another mustard armchair and a coffee table where a sheet of paper, a pack of cigarettes and a pile of money lay. Cassie reached for the paper and a sharp pain darted up her arm. It was bruised – purple, red and blue. She reached again, slower this time, and retrieved the paper – a handwritten note on headed notepaper:

The Alexander Hotel. Dublin 4. Five stars.

In an instant, the night flashed before her. Jeff, a good-looking man (or was it John?) on a stag night for his friend Dave. (Dylan? Dev?) English. Nice guy, from what she could remember. A dark bar. Dancing. Lap dancing? Falling, fighting, taxi, sex? Yes. Lots of sex. Screaming? There was a black hole where this information should be, but her gut warned not to scratch at that scab. The light hurt her eyes and so she closed one eye and read on.

Dear Cassie,

Last night was great, you're a legend. We're gone back on the early flight. Sleep on, you don't have to be out until 11 a.m. and have a drink at the bar before you go.
Jeff and John. And especially Dev (but don't tell his fiancée).

Cassie ran to the toilet and vomited until there was nothing left. Dragging herself off the bathroom floor, she crawled back to bed on her hand and knees and gagged again. At least the days of needing emergency contraception were gone. Two glass bottles of Icelandic water stood on a crystal tray under the plasma TV, which she fetched and gulped down, then switched on the TV. Morning TV. 8:15 a.m. – a few more hours before she had to leave, a few more hours with a bed.

An image of the three men flashed in her mind, but she couldn't think about that now. The room was too hot, the pillows too soft and her head too sore. She needed to sleep.

Tara. Her sister. So pretty and well dressed, if she remembered rightly. Well-off too. She tossed and turned but, with no sign of sleep coming, Cassie eased herself into the black rainfall shower, letting the water fall over her aching muscles and stifling a wail when each hot drop hit the grazed insides of her arms and thighs. She stayed under the water until her skin shrivelled and wrinkled, then stepped out onto heated tiles and wrapped herself in a plush white bath towel. A good wash normally did wonders for her mood after a heavy drinking session, but not today. At least she had her holdall, and a change of clothes into something clean would help. Barefoot on the light patterned carpet, she searched for her bag to no avail. She kneeled to check under the bed, when a fresh blood stain on the carpet triggered a snapshot memory accompanied by an English voice.

"Come on, mate. You've had your turn, leave some for the rest of us."

Cassie lay on the floor, curled her knees to her chest and sobbed. What a mess. Everything she touched turned bad.

A drink, that's what she needed. A drink at the bar to steady the nerves; help her think straight. She'd need clean clothes for that, where was her bag?

She remembered having it in the off-licence, because she put the litre bottle of vodka into it. In St Stephen's Green? Yes, at first, but her memory grew sketchier as the day went on. She could ask Tara if she had it when they met, but shame filled her when she thought of their encounter. The hotel would have WiFi; she should hop onto it and message Tara to apologise for her behaviour, then ask about her bag. She opened the heavy embroidered curtains and the morning light flooded the room, blinding her. She searched the room again, then checked in the pockets of her coat. Her phone was gone too.

She really needed that drink. The cupboard under the TV caught her eye. A minibar! She opened the door, but it was a tea and coffee station, along with a kettle, sachets of sugar and powdered milk.

Room service ran 24/7. She'd been in enough hotels to know that. She dialled 'bar service' from the hotel landline. An automated message played. "Due to industry-wide staff shortages, our room service menu is not available until midday. Please visit Claude's, our award-winning bar on the ground floor, from 10:30 a.m., where you will find a deluxe range of—"

Cassie slammed the phone down and banged it repeatedly in its cradle. She'd have to go to the bar, which meant getting back in her clothes from last night. She collected her dirty, wet clothes from around the room and put them on, then checked the cigarette box. One left. She'd smoke that outside before going to the bar to steady the nerves.

She left the room, taking the key with her. Noting the number, she smiled at a couple coming towards her in the narrow corridor, but they blanked her, looked into the distance and continued walking. Outside the front of the hotel, she smoked the last cigarette in the cold as traffic built on the road beside her, heading into the city centre.

Christmas music played in the warm and cosy bar. She called a double vodka and Coke from the clean-shaven barman in a white starched shirt and fitted wine waistcoat stocking the shelves. He barely registered her but pushed a long glass under the optic of the unturned bottle of vodka, releasing the clear liquid.

"Ice and lemon?" he asked.

"Please." She couldn't care less about ice and lemon but wanted to appear nonchalant, like this was no big deal, like it wasn't going to be the highlight of her day. If she played her cards right, this would be the first of many.

"Room number?"

"Two one five."

He stopped pouring and turned to look at her. "One moment, madam." Disappearing through the back of the bar, he returned with a smaller, rounder man in a black suit who looked at Cassie like she was shit on his shoe. "I'm afraid this bar is closed, Miss."

"But you just opened."

"I said it's closed. Please leave. I will personally show you out."

He escorted Cassie onto the street. "Your behaviour last night was unacceptable. We have families staying here, Miss. We are not that kind of establishment. Please never come back to these premises again." He turned on his heels and returned to the warmth of the bar.

A dreadlocked passer-by stared at Cassie. "Have you a spare cigarette, hun?" she asked, and he obliged, lighting it for her. "It's the system," he said. "It's screwed up."

"Thanks, man." She inhaled deeply. *Think, Cassie. Think.*

Rummaging through her coat pockets again, she touched something in the lining. She manipulated her fingers and grasped the corner of a soft, pliable square, pulling it out through the hole.

A wallet.

9

TARA

Tara barely had her coat off when she felt a presence loom over her. Joan in a jumpsuit. With eyes bulging, her black hair pulled off her face into a ponytail and lips even redder than normal, she looked insane.

"I need a word. Now." She turned on her heels, not waiting for an answer.

Tara followed her into a meeting room and Joan slammed the door behind her, pulling the venetian blinds on the window shut with a snap. This was not going to be pleasant.

"Where did you go yesterday and why did you not answer your phone? You know your figures were all wrong, right? You had the data locked to your username. Thanks to you, we missed our project deadline. The whole team missed their deadline, meaning we all missed our bonus. All you had to do was pick up your bloody phone, or carry the one we gave you."

Tara's heart skipped a beat. "Sorry, it was an accident. I'd a headache and had to leave. I had my phone on mute."

Joan stepped back and drank in the whole of Tara, then laughed. "Did this headache come on at the hairdresser's, by any chance?"

Tara said nothing, focusing on her boots and hoping an answer would come. Either that or Joan would get tired waiting and continue giving out.

"I asked you a question." A vein throbbed in Joan's right temple like Mother's did when she was angry. Oh boy, you did not want to make Mother angry. "Hello? I'm waiting!"

Tara couldn't think. "Sorry, what was the question?"

Joan threw her hands up. "Unbelievable. I can't deal with this, with you! How did I ever end up with you on my team? You ... you ... you ...you know, I think you do this on purpose, I don't think you are as innocent as you make out." She stomped out of the room, leaving the door open. When she didn't come back after a few minutes, Tara returned to her desk and popped two painkillers as a precaution.

There was so much to do, but her head was not on her work or the daggers she was getting from everyone in the office. It was on her sister. Where was she? Tara left her on the streets with no money and in no fit state to look after herself. Oh God, that was a terrible thing to do. All she'd ever wanted was a sister. Someone to share games and stories with. Someone to play and fight with, to have her back. As an adult, she often wished for someone to help with Mother, to help share the load. Not that she resented going over every night. No way. Mary had looked after her, schooled her, cared for her since she was born – it was Tara's turn now. But sometimes, after a hard day or when she didn't feel up to it, on days when she wanted to slip between the sheets and shut the world out, on those nights, it would have been nice to have someone to take over.

She should call the police. Anything could have happened to Cassie. She didn't even care if she had taken the wallet, which was a possibility, but those youths could have nicked it when they pushed against her, or she could have left it in the bar. She was certainly tipsy enough. Tara said nothing this morning when Barry scanned her in and held the door open for her but she'd have to report her work ID missing today. She could say she lost it, although Mother always said it wasn't good to tell lies.

"Oh, what a tangled web we weave when first we practise to deceive," she'd say. A quote from Shakespeare's *Macbeth* – no, Walter Scott's *Marmion*. Both writers studied in their school for one. Tara always tried to tell the truth, but when she did, it seemed to irritate people, so sometimes she lied for their benefit.

The morning dragged on and by midday her concentration was shot. Her colleagues were making it their business to huff and puff as they passed, her head was full of dilemmas and her stomach roared. Without breakfast this morning, or Mother's cherry scones for elevenses, she'd had nothing to eat since last night.

Mother. She should have told her about Cassie, but the doctor warned absolutely no upsets or change and all those reports of Cherish the Child on TV showing heartbroken women – she couldn't do that to her. For a woman in her eighties, she was doing well mentally but she had been growing frail in front of Tara's eyes, colds and chest infections taking longer, with more antibiotics and steroids, to clear.

Something must have happened to make her give up her

baby. From the news, it was clear that back then society shamed mothers who got pregnant outside of wedlock. Maybe she'd felt too ashamed to tell her, but Tara wouldn't have judged her. She would have understood and never broken her confidence.

What was Cassie's life like? Had she been sold to the highest bidder and, if so, was it to someone decent? No, it was pretty obvious it wasn't. Tara's tummy roared. She needed to eat.

The basement canteen was noisy and hot. Tara took a tray and queued along the hot food counter. Everything was fried in batter or covered in butter. She passed the steaming food, the deli counter, the prepacked sandwiches and finally the desserts and pastries before returning the tray to its bay. She could survive until tonight. Only a few hours more to go.

At the coffee station, Tara chose her mug with the logo *All you need is love and good coffee* and selected Americano on the automated display. The machine churned into action and she held the mug under the tap as the coffee flowed.

Bam! Someone bumped into her, knocking the mug out of her hands, the black liquid scalding her hand and drenching her skirt. The mug hit the floor and smashed into pieces. She looked up to see Joan smirking.

"Sorry, it was an accident," Joan said and walked away.

Tara picked up the pieces of her mug in silence, alone in the packed canteen. That was her favourite mug, the one Mary bought for her last Christmas. She seethed and muttered the rhyme her mother had taught her through gritted teeth.

Sticks and stones may break my bones,
but names will never hurt me.
When I'm gone, and in my grave

you'll suffer for what you called me.

With a fresh coffee in a polystyrene cup, she returned to her desk and checked her email.

Dear Tara,

I am delighted to invite you to interview for the role of Customer Liaison Team Lead, tomorrow at 10 a.m. in the Lir Suite, Floor 4.

Please confirm your attendance by return mail.

Kind regards,
Matt Jordan
Customer Experience Manager

Her hand still stung from the coffee and Tara thought of wiping the smile off Joan's smug face if she got the job, making her the same grade as her. Joan looked down her nose at her, treating her like dirt. The adrenaline pumped hard and she hit reply.

Dear Matt,

I am delighted to confirm I will be at the interview tomorrow morning at 10 a.m.

Kind regards,
Tara Ryan
Data Analysis Clerk

She checked her workload, the fresh nail imprints on her

palms tingling. Four projects had been assigned to her in the last few minutes by Joan, four irrelevant pieces of work that nobody else wanted. She sighed, took a deep breath and opened the first project. There was no point in complaining; she'd have the work done in the same time. By late afternoon, she was well stuck in when the phone on her desk rang.

"Tara, it's Fee in Reception. There's a, ahem, lady here to see you." It was hard to hear her voice over the shouting in the background.

"Sorry, Fee, *who* is there to see me?"

"A woman called Cassandra Blake." The noise was punctured by a shrill scream. "Come quickly, she's causing a scene."

10

CASSIE

"I need to talk to Tara Ryan. Let me in."

A security guard in bulletproof vest blocked the rotating glass door to the fancy five-storey Partners Plus building in the Grand Canal Dock business district.

"Sorry, love, not without access permission. This is a high-security premises. I told you that already."

Inside the glass-fronted building, sharply dressed twenty-somethings in folded-arm groups judged her from the foot of the waterfall that began on the fifth floor. She knew how she looked to them in her dirty clothes, and she hated it, but she needed to speak to Tara.

It was easy to find this place. The work ID in Tara's wallet had the name of the company and all Cassie had to do was ask for directions. Everyone seemed to know the company and where it was. Now, this asshole was the only thing stopping her from gaining access. There was probably ten times worse than her in the boardroom in there and, if she was wearing clean clothes, she bet she wouldn't have been stopped. But dirty and desperate, she kept that to herself. She needed to see Tara urgently.

"Cassie?" A woman who looked almost as out of place here as Cassie did, stood at the glass door, the security guard blocking her exit. Cassie squinted. Was it? Oh God, it was. It was Tara! She must have been drunker than she thought last night because she remembered a beautiful, stylish woman, not this ... this run-down frump in a stained, shapeless skirt and sensible boots. She was like something from *Little House on the Prairie*. A woman that time forgot – or, more precisely, something from a nunnery.

The security guard turned to Tara. "You know this woman?"

She nodded. "Yes, she's an ... an acquaintance. What's going on?"

Acquaintance. *Ouch*. Cassie let it go and approached the door but the security guard took a step towards her. By now, a crowd had gathered outside too, as unimpressed workers waited to re-enter the building.

"I just want to talk to her," Cassie cried. "Why won't you let me in?"

He stood firm. "Are you stupid? I told you already nobody is allowed into this building without authorisation and a valid ID. Do you have authorisation or a valid ID? No. So, you're not getting in. *Comprendez?*"

Cassie had an access card in her pocket, just not belonging to her, and a wallet she needed to return. "You didn't stop anyone else going in. Why me? Come on, two minutes. Please?"

"You're not coming in and that's the end of it. If you want to talk, you can go someplace else. Now, step aside and let these good people past."

Tara walked out past the security guard and the current of people now filing into the building.

"Are you drunk?" she asked. "Are you on something?"

"No, nothing. I'm sober. I haven't had a drink all day."

Tara stared at her for ages before nodding. "Okay. Can you hold on a minute while I get my bag and coat? We can go grab a coffee."

A black-haired woman walking into the building turned on her heels. "No, Tara. No. We have an important meeting in two minutes. You're going nowhere."

Tara looked like a little puppy and something inside Cassie rose up, making her want to punch the woman in the face.

Who do you think you are? she wanted to ask the woman with the pursed red lips, but Tara looked embarrassed and the situation was already elevated. Not the time, or the place. She swallowed her words.

Tara offered Cassie a smile. "I'd better stay here for now but I finish in an hour, can you come back then?"

No, Tara didn't understand. Cassie couldn't wait. If she held onto the wallet any longer, she'd spend the contents. It had taken all her resolve to get here with it intact. She'd passed countless pubs, supermarkets, shops, restaurants and off-licences. She'd sat for hours over a pot of tea, deciding what to do. If she spent the money, she'd get the drink she craved with her soul but she'd be back at square one tomorrow. If she returned it, Tara may want nothing to do with her, and it could be for nothing, but what if she forgave her? What if she let her into her life?

This was a one-time-only offer, her only chance.

"It can't wait, hun. I need to talk to you now. It's urgent."

The black-haired woman crossed her arms. "Tara! Inside. Now!"

Tara stood between both women, looking from one to the other.

"Tara," the woman spat. "I'm warning you. If you don't come inside this minute, I will report you. Your work has been sub-par and you are skating on thin ice."

Tara clenched both fists, like she was going to punch the woman, who took a step back as if feeling it too.

"Wait there, Cassie," Tara said. "I'll be out in two minutes."

11

TARA

Cassie was perched on the raised brick flowerbed outside the building, smoking a cigarette, when Tara returned a few minutes later. She knew Joan would make trouble for her after disappearing yesterday and now doing it again, but those projects she gave her were languishing for months with no urgency and this was far more important. She never took a day off or a holiday or even called in sick. She never rocked the boat in work, even though there were many times she had reason to. No, she could report all she liked, she hadn't a leg to stand on.

Cassie's hands trembled as she raised the cigarette to her lips again. She was a mess, even worse than Tara remembered, and she had on the same clothes as the night before. At least she was alive, though, and for that Tara was grateful.

Cassie stubbed out her cigarette. "I appreciate you doing this, hun."

"No problem. How did you find me?"

Cassie took out her wallet and Tara's heart sank.

"Your work ID. I asked around where Partners Plus was.

It wasn't hard with those—" She looked up to the brass balls hanging from the red-brick building. "Talk about a man's world."

Tara examined the wallet. It was hers alright and, although she was grateful for its return, the fact remained Cassie had stolen it from her. Everything seemed to be there, including the cash.

"I found it in my coat this morning," Cassie said, "but I swear I have no memory of taking it. If I did, I'd have spent the money last night, but when I found it this morning I was faced with a dilemma – take the money and throw away the wallet, pretending I never saw it, or return it to you. I chose the second."

"Thank you for doing the right thing," Tara said.

"No, don't thank me. I was this close," she made a gap between her forefinger and thumb, "this close to spending it on booze. So many times. Please don't thank me."

Tara was confused. Now she was feeling sorry for the woman who stole her wallet? "But you did the right thing in the end, that has to matter."

"Last night ..." Cassie's voice caught and she trailed off as Barry turned the corner.

"Tara, is everything okay?" he asked, eyeballing Cassie.

"It's fine, but I have to go," she said. "There's an emergency. I'll explain tomorrow morning."

"Really, Tara? After yesterday?" He inhaled deeply and continued up the steps. Even Barry was annoyed with her.

"We should move away from here," Tara said.

"Last night was something I never want to repeat," Cassie said, as they strolled down the street away from Partners Plus. "This behaviour has to stop – I have to stop, before it's too late."

"What exactly happened last night?" Tara asked.

"I can't even think about ... Jesus Christ, I just found you and I robbed you, and then the men." Cassie stopped and faced her. "I don't want to be this person. I want to be better, to know about your life. You're my little sister. I'm supposed to look after you and instead I take from you. I can't even look after myself."

Tara felt a lump in her throat. Cassie, her sister, wanted to look out for her. "Have you eaten?"

Cassie sniffled. "No, but don't give me money. Please."

"I won't. There's a café down here. It's a bit pretentious but it's nice. If you like, I could buy you something to eat and we could chat for a bit, but I don't have long. I'm having dinner with my – our – mother tonight and, besides, you probably have to get back to Mayo."

"Thank you. That's really kind of you and, no, I don't have to get back to Mayo. I have nowhere and no one to go back to."

She was homeless. This wasn't good.

"Kitchen's closing soon," the bearded waiter said. Tara asked for a coffee as Cassie scanned the menu again, eventually settling on the lasagne, chips and a can of Coke.

With their orders placed, Cassie leaned across the table in the otherwise empty café and took a deep breath. "This is awkward. Did I have a bag with me yesterday when I met you? A black holdall?"

Tara thought back to Cassie lying on the ground outside Brooke's, screaming at the security man. There was no bag. "No, not that I remember."

Cassie put her head in her trembling hands. "Great. Just great. My whole life was in there."

The waiter in the half apron returned with their drinks

balanced on a tray and sighed when he poured Cassie's cola over the rocks of ice in the tall glass, like the very thought of it offended him.

"I appreciate this so much. Thank you," Cassie said, gulping down most of her drink in one go. "I don't think they're too happy to have the likes of me here."

"I don't think it's you. They probably want to close up, time is getting on," Tara said, but now she mentioned it, the staff were whispering and staring in their direction. She looked at Cassie again and reality sobered her up. She was a wreck.

When the food came, Cassie polished off her chips and dived into the lasagne. Tara watched her eat with one eye on the clock. It was 5:30 p.m. Too late to catch the 5:40 p.m. train, but there was one every ten minutes. She still had time to get to Mary's for dinner, but she had to go home to change her clothes first. Mother would be disgusted if she showed up for dinner with that coffee stain on her skirt.

Cassie stopped eating and pushed the lasagne away. She'd turned a strange shade of green. "I think I have had enough," she said and took a large gulp from her remaining Coke and let out a loud burp.

The waiter glared over and Tara didn't know what to say. "Maybe we should leave—"

"Can we talk about what we're both here for?" Cassie asked. "You're my sister and I am yours and I cannot believe I just said that."

Tara couldn't believe it either and yet it was happening. "I had no idea I had a sister. I thought I was an only child until yesterday. I think I am in shock."

"It is a huge shock," Cassie agreed. "How should we do this? You go first? Tell me about you."

Tara was taken aback. She didn't often get asked to talk about herself. "Me? Uhm, I was born and raised in Cushla, a small town on the coast of North County Dublin. Live on my own, not married, no kids, no pets." It sounded so boring.

"Amazing," Cassie said. "You have it all."

Tara smiled. That was not the reaction she expected. "I suppose you are right; I have been very lucky."

"And you grew up there?"

Tara nodded.

Cassie swallowed. "Were you happy?" she asked after a moment.

"Yes, I was. I was very happy. Our parents, Mary and Frank Ryan, got married a few years after you were born, and Mother got pregnant then a year later with me. I – we – never had more siblings, although I always wanted one."

Cassie's mouth was open and Tara realised she was being insensitive talking about family life. "I'm sure they would have kept you too if they could; they were good people."

Cassie raised her eyebrows and went to say something but stopped, sitting back in her chair "You mean Mary and Frank are your biological parents? You weren't adopted?"

Tara looked confused. "What? Oh no, they're my – our – biological parents. I'm sorry, it must be hard knowing I got to live with them while they gave you up."

"I want to meet them," Cassie said.

"I'm afraid Daddy died a long time ago in a car crash that left Mother in a wheelchair. She is very sick, so I don't want to involve her in this. Not yet anyway."

Cassie whistled. "That's terrible. I'm so sorry to hear that, but it's impossible to not involve her in this – it's her that did all this. She's already involved."

Tara leaned in. "Mother's dying. Every day we get

together is a blessing; she can't be stressed out. Doctor Lucas was very clear on that. No upset."

There were tears in Cassie's eyes, but she didn't answer.

"Mother is hard work but she is a good person. Honestly. They were different times back then, that's all I know. I'm sure whatever she did was with a good heart."

Cassie's lip wobbled but she still didn't speak. It was like she was frozen in time.

"Maybe it was like those arrangements in the Cherish the Child story," Tara said. "You know, that they wanted to find you but signed something like an NDA to say they wouldn't. Have you seen it on the news?"

"Seen it?" Cassie spat, breaking her silence. "I lived it! Where do you think I grew up?"

"Oh no, not an orphanage." Tara's stomach dropped as she said the word. "Oh God, I'm so sorry, and there's me going on about my life."

"It wasn't your fault."

"What was it like there?" Tara felt sick. She hoped Cassie would say it was a decent place to grow up in and that all her needs were met. She hoped she'd say she was well looked after by kind staff, but instead she just shook her head.

The waiter paced, making little effort to hide his irritation, and Tara checked her phone. It was 5:50 p.m. and she'd missed the train again. She needed to get moving if she was going to make dinner at all, but she felt so sad for the woman sitting opposite her that nothing else seemed to matter.

"I was born in Mayo, near the CTC home," Cassie said, ignoring the waiter. "I grew up in the system, with no family. Well, there was one who took pity on me when I was small. Mrs Graham. A lovely woman, like a mother to me, but her family didn't want me and so they sent me back to the home. I was still living there when I aged out of the system at sixteen."

"That's terrible."

Cassie raised an eyebrow. "You have no idea. It was hell on earth. Anyway, there you have it. You had a good life and I had a shit one. Tale as old as time. Poor alcoholic, she always has a bleeding-heart story, but probably lies as always." She looked hard at Tara. "You can't trust the Lord's prayer out of an alco's mouth, right?"

"Are you an alcoholic?" Tara whispered, already knowing the answer.

"Yes, I suppose I am." Cassie nodded, a look on her face that Tara couldn't quite read. "And that is the first time I've really admitted it. My name is Cassie Blake and I am an alcoholic. I've tried giving up so many times, and I can go for long stretches without touching a drop, but it always calls me back. Before this slip I was over three months off the drink. I thought I was safe, but that's the thing with addiction. It's always waiting to bite you in the ass. Last night was rock bottom." She looked at her dirty runners and chewed her fingernails. "Can I ask a favour? Could you buy me cigarettes?"

With the returned wallet in her pocket, Tara supposed it was the right thing to do after leaving Cassie in such a state the night before with nowhere to go. She checked her watch. If she left now, she'd make the 6:20 p.m. train. "I'll buy them for you but then I have to go. I am so late for dinner," she said.

"Can you text your mam to say you're running late?" Cassie asked.

"Yes," Tara admitted, as she wrote a quick message and

sent it. "But Mother worries if I'm late and she's not supposed to have any upsets, so I'd like to get there ASAP."

Cassie stood up and the waiter swiped the plate from under her nose. "Where does Mary live?"

"You can call her Mother – she's your mother too."

"Nope, she'll never be my mam," Cassie said. "I'll stick with Mary, thanks all the same."

Tara wasn't surprised. She couldn't even imagine how it must feel to be abandoned by your own parents. It made sense that Cassie was reluctant to call this woman she hadn't even met yet Mother. A mother should care for their child, above all others. She remembered the verse in the card she gave Mary last Mother's Day:

A Mother's love is always there
To wipe your tears and show she cares.
A mother puts her child above
Her own needs, that's a mother's love.

"Hello?" Cassie's voice interrupted her thoughts. "Where does your mam live?"

"Oh, sorry. She lives in Cushla too. Right across the road from my place."

Cassie put her coat on. "Come on so, let's go. We can talk and walk. There's something you should know about your parents."

C assie stood in front of Tara's apartment building, lost for words.

She'd managed to persuade Tara to buy her a train ticket and then walked home with her from the station, holding off Tara's questioning about what Cassie needed to tell her until they'd reached her home. Cassie felt a little bad about forcing her presence on her sister, but she had nowhere else to go and Tara, though seemingly reluctant, hadn't stopped her. And now she was here.

She hadn't gawped as they left the train station and entered the most idyllic neighbourhood she'd ever seen. She didn't gasp as they passed the pretty houses lining both sides of the hill or the quaint bakeries and cafés, but this was unreal. An apartment right in the harbour.

"You live here? It's a palace! You must have some rent!"

"No, I don't pay any rent. Mother bought it for me out of Daddy's settlement. We got a huge life assurance pay out when he passed – like millions – so she paid her own house off and bought me this. Now, what was it you wanted to tell me?"

Cassie thought of Sharon's words.

Your problem is you just dive in. You don't think of the consequences.

"What is it?" Tara asked again. "What did you want to tell me?"

The gates of the complex opened and a black sports car rumbled out through them.

Two properties. Mary owned one too, and she was dying.

You don't understand the concept of delayed gratification, of waiting that bit longer, of having patience for a far greater result.

Tara's version of events in the café earlier had taken her by surprise. It seemed that Tara truly thought her parents were their biological parents, that they had given Cassie away.

It was far from the truth.

But Sharon was right. And something had told Cassie to stay quiet. Now, standing in front of Tara's luxurious home, she was glad she had.

No, this was not the time to tell Tara the truth; that she had it all wrong. It was not the time to tell her that Mary wasn't their mother at all.

Not the time to tell her that it wasn't Cassie who had been taken.

13

CASSIE

Before

It was a sunny day in summer. She knew that because she remembered the mud was dry under her bare feet and her lightest dress, the one They brought the last time They visited, was stuck to her. It was bright blue at first, but it had faded and was tight across her back now. Playing outside to distract herself from the crying baby in the house, she wished her mammy would wake up.

Mammy often went to bed in the daytime while Cassie played in the cornfields, which was grand before the baby came, but not anymore. The baby needed her milk.

Cassie had tried to help, picking the screaming baby up, careful to cradle her under the head. She put her finger in the baby's mouth, but she pushed it back out with her tongue and howled. She was hungry for Mammy's milk. Cassie was hungry too, but she was used to it.

She carried the distressed baby to her mammy's bedroom. It was dark, the curtains closed and it smelled like that time she got sick. "Mammy, please wake up, the baby needs your milk," she said, but Mammy didn't move, the covers pulled up over her head. Cassie shook her, but she wouldn't wake up. An empty bottle lay on the floor beside her bed and white pills were scattered all over the floor.

Cassie didn't know she was dead, but she did know something was very wrong. She wasn't supposed to leave the fields, but she laced up the shoes They brought that squeezed her toes and made for the farmhouse over the hill where she had watched the family, wishing she could live with them. They were like the Ingalls from *Little House on the Prairie*, she thought. Perfect.

She was running as fast as her little legs could carry her when the sound of tyres on the dirt road hit her. She stopped and ducked down, in time to see a woman in a red car pass by and head towards the end of the lane, where only their house was. It was a small car – a Mini maybe, one that looked like it was smiling at you.

She watched the woman's feet in high, laced brown shoes with wooden heels enter the house, then come out with the baby, still screaming. She opened the back door of the car and, when she closed it again, the cries had stopped. Then, she got into the red car and drove off. That was the last time Cassie ever saw her sister. She should have stopped her, but she couldn't move. She should have screamed not to take the baby but her whole body froze as the woman took her away.

When the car was long gone, Cassie found her strength and ran all the way to the farmhouse over the hill to the perfect family. The mammy brought her in and gave her biscuits and a glass of orange. She remembered because that

was her first time having either of them and they were
sweeter than the blackberries that grew in the ditches.

Lots of Them came then, saying her mammy was gone to
heaven and asking where her father was. She didn't have a
daddy, so asked if she could stay with the perfect family. She
guessed the answer was no because They took her to
Cherish the Child that night.

Imagining things.

When she told them about the woman taking her baby
sister, they said she was imagining things. There was no
baby. The more Cassie insisted, kicking up murder, the more
she was punished. She learnt quickly to keep it inside,
turning memories to dreams. They said if she couldn't
behave, she'd never get a family.

Over the years Cassie returned to the house where she
once lived many times. Nobody ever moved in and she
watched as it gradually started to fall down, becoming more
and more derelict. The weeds grew so high in the dirt road
no car could get in. Ivy grew up the stone walls that crum-
bled at the edges and the roof slowly collapsed and was
reclaimed by wildlife. And inside was even worse: over the
years, the house became a site for parties and fires, the orig-
inal furniture still in place but vandalised and abused, her
mother's bed sodden.

It was Sharon who first suggested Cassie take a DNA test,
offering to pay. It was something other people she'd previously helped had really valued, she'd said, a chance to find
family, to reconnect. To find those that might have been lost
in the chaos of care homes, broken lives and alcoholism.

And, once again, Sharon had been right.

14

TARA

Tara stopped outside the complex and turned to Cassie. "Right, so ... uhm, thanks for walking me home. Did you think what it was you wanted to tell me?"

Cassie leaned against the perimeter wall. "What?"

"You said you wanted to tell me something important."

Cassie shrugged. "Oh sorry, I've forgotten what it was, must have been a lie." She grinned. "Just kidding, more like memory loss – all part of the hangover process, hun. Terrible it is. Never drink, that's my advice."

She lit up a cigarette, showing no sign of leaving. Tara didn't want to be rude, but time was moving on and she hoped Cassie didn't think she could stay here. There only one bedroom for a start, but it was more than that. This woman made her nervous.

Cassie surveyed her surrounds. "This place is beautiful; I can only imagine what it's like in the daytime. The harbour, the sea, the houses, it's all gorgeous. It must be so nice to come home here every night."

Tara hadn't thought about it, but now that she mentioned it, yes – it was nice. The neighbours were quiet and nobody ever bothered her.

Cassie crossed the pedestrian walkway and leaned over the metal chains that hung from the blue boulders. "A walkway along the seafront too? How far does it go before you have to come up off the seafront?"

"I think it goes to Portmarnock, but I don't know. I've never walked it."

"I'd never be off it if I lived here." Cassie stubbed out her cigarette and danced a little jig. "I shouldn't have drunk all that Coke. I'm bursting. Would you mind if I used your loo?"

Tara's heart thumped. She knew what was happening but how could she refuse anyone, let alone her sister, the use of her toilet? "You can use it, but you have to be quick or I'll be late for dinner. I'm literally changing my clothes and leaving."

Cassie's shoulders slumped. Tara understood. This was her home, yet Cassie had nothing. It seemed so unfair, considering they had the same blood. It had to be tough on her, but still, she wanted her gone. "What are you doing tomorrow?" she asked.

"No plans." Cassie said. "Tara, hun, I hate to ask, honestly I do, but I have nowhere to go tonight and I'm afraid if I go back into the city, I'll rob, get drunk and something terrible will happen to me. Can I stay with you? I promise I will be gone first thing in the morning. One night while I get my head together. Please."

Tara stiffened, pulling her coat around her. Cassie was her sister, but she had also robbed her, was homeless and an alcoholic. "The apartment is a one-bed."

"I'll sleep on your couch. I'll sleep anywhere."

She bit her lip. "I don't think it's a good idea."

"Please. I'm desperate. I need a shower, I'm exhausted and have nowhere to go. Please?" Cassie pulled her hood up and shivered in the freezing wind.

Tara was stuck. On one hand, Cassie was her sister and in need of help. On the other, she was a mess. Tara had to make a decision quickly and the pressure of Cassie's pleading eyes didn't help. The outside of her vision began to swim.

"Okay," she said before a migraine set in, "but just for tonight."

Cassie threw her arms around her. "You're a lifesaver."

Tara tapped her back, trying to block out the doubts that were screaming at her along with the putrid smell of Cassie's hair.

What was she doing, letting a stranger into her home, especially one like this? If someone told her on Tuesday she'd be here, considering this, she would have thought they were quite mad, but a lot had happened since then and it wasn't like she had a choice. Mother would freak out, but she always said family came above everything, that nothing else matters – work, money, holidays, even friends. Once you have family, Mother would say, you have everything, and Cassie was family.

She shaded the keypad with her hand and punched in the access code. The electronic gates opened and Cassie followed her to the entrance of her building, where she punched in a different code and the door opened with a high-pitched tone.

They passed the massive Christmas tree in the white marble foyer, entered the lift and Tara pressed the button for the sixth floor.

Cassie's eyes widened. "The penthouse? Wow."

"One night," Tara said, unlocking her front door and turning off the alarm.

"One night," Cassie repeated, stepping into the apartment.

15

CASSIE

She kept her head down as they made their way to the penthouse – *Penthouse!* – apartment. It was like Fort Knox with all the locks, but when Tara opened the door and switched on the light to reveal a huge, open-plan room in a flat which must have cost a small fortune, Cassie gagged. It was musty and drab with clothes strewn everywhere. A breakfast bowl with caked cereal sat on the kitchen table, glasses and dishes lay unwashed on the counter and the sink was full to the brim with uncovered food all around on the work surfaces. This place was a dump.

Tara drew the full-length cream curtains on the massive windows.

"Sorry about the state of the place. I hate cleaning so I only do basic housekeeping on Saturdays," Tara said, like it was no big deal. If Cassie lived here, she'd have the place spotless. Hold on ...

"Tara, hun, if it's okay with you, I'll clean up the place while you're at your ma's. I really enjoy housework and it would be my way of saying thanks for letting me stay tonight."

"But you said you need a shower and you're tired." Tara scrunched up her nose. "And Saturday is when I clean."

"Well, maybe you could do something else on Saturday? Something nicer? Besides I'll sleep well tonight then, and it'd be my way of thanking you."

Tara considered for a moment. "Okay, but don't go into my room. You're still a stranger and you did take my wallet."

It was kind of refreshing, her honesty. She was almost funny, but nothing seemed smart or calculated like the girls Cassie had grown up with. Was she a bit simple? Or was it innocence? Cassie couldn't figure it out.

Tara changed her clothes, returning in a black skirt, equally as drab and dowdy, and with folded flannelette pyjamas that she handed to Cassie. "You can wear these, there are towels and toiletries in the bathroom. I'll be back by ten. Would you like me to pick you up something? I always go to the corner shop on my way home."

"If you would like me to cook breakfast in the morning, get the full works. It would be my pleasure."

Tara looked confused, like she didn't know what went into a fry-up, so Cassie listed the components out. "Sausages, rashers, eggs, black pudding, tomatoes, beans, bread, the lot, and if you don't mind can you get me cigarettes and a bottle of Coke?"

"But I bought you cigarettes ... of course, I'll get them." Tara looked concerned. "You can't smoke in here, though, there's an alarm. You have to go out on the balcony."

Cassie pulled the curtain back to see an ample balcony outside. "No problem, out there is perfect."

"Get back!" Tara hissed. "Mother will see you."

"Your mother? From here?" Cassie peeped out and into the back gardens below. Long narrow gardens and terraced houses with smoke rising from the chimneys. What sort of an arrangement was this, living so close to each other?

"She lives in the houses to your right. You can see into her back garden from the balcony, meaning she can also see us. Obviously. I haven't mentioned you yet and the doctor says no surprises, so please stay inside until I come back. I'll show you where I keep the cleaning stuff."

Cassie followed Tara into the kitchen area, where she opened the cupboard door, hanging off its hinges, to reveal a heap of cleaning products. Then, with an uncertain smile, Tara left.

Cassie exhaled. First, she took a long hot shower, the cuts and bruises already feeling better. Then she put on the pyjamas Tara gave her, having to pull the string on the waist to its tightest to keep them from falling down. Finally, she made a cup of instant black coffee. She liked it milky, but there was none in the fridge. There was nothing in the fridge except for a couple of almost empty wine bottles, which she tried to ignore, and some shrivelled grapes, yet it still smelled, and looked, grimy.

It was such a waste; this place could be really nice if it was looked after. She tore a black sack from its roll and got stuck into tidying up.

There's wine in the fridge.

Cassie ignored the thought and turned on the TV in the living room, surfing channels for anything to ground her back to the present.

She found TV News 24/7.

Shauna Murray is a recently graduated primary school teacher, working in a school in West Dublin. She shares a house with three other teachers and their lease is about to expire. The landlord has indicated he will increase the rent by €1,000 per month. With this news, Shauna has made a tough decision.

"Yeah, it's totally not doable, and I don't want to, but I have to go to Dubai. It's a shame because I want to stay here, my girl-friend is here and so is my family, but I don't have any other option. There aren't enough houses for people to live in anymore."

Cassie turned it off; she didn't need to be reminded about the shortage of housing. She cleaned the living area, kitchen and continued down the hall, stopping outside Tara's bedroom. The door was ajar and she pushed it to see an unholy mess with an unmade double bed.

Sharon in Dignity House would have had a fit.

Make your bed every morning. No excuses, no exceptions, she said. *Tidy room, tidy mind.*

Clothes and books were scattered on the stained beige carpet and the smell was like that of the old hostels she had stayed in by the sea. Musty or fusty, she couldn't remember which one. Rotten anyway, like a cross between a nursing home and a school changing room, with an undertow of feet. Towels were strewn on top of the bed and boxes of stuff lined the walls. How did one person make such a mess and what exactly did Tara clean on a Saturday?

She wondered about Mary's house. What was that like? Maybe she could help out there too. If she could make herself useful, they might keep her around a bit longer and with the old lady already dying ...

Well, everything might work out.

16

I t was 7 p.m. by the time Tara got to Mary's house, thirty minutes late. The smell of hot fat made her tummy growl. She hadn't eaten all day apart from that tiny café brownie and Thursday was fish and chips day – smoked cod, homemade chips and baked beans. Tara adored this meal as a child and she would die for it now, she was so hungry.

"It's me," she called from the hallway, bending to give Marmalade a pet. Sooty sidled in on her other side and the two cats stretched out on their backs at her feet.

"It's not a bad evening out there," she called, giving the cats a good rub, but their purring was the only response. For a terrible moment she imagined the worst – Mary lying dead on the living-room floor. She dashed into the living room, where Mary sat at the dining table clasping a string of rosary beads, her eyes closed and lips moving in silent prayer. A basket of chips, a bowl of coagulated baked beans and two pieces of cod, that Snowy was sniffing, lay on the table.

Tara picked the cat up off the table, but he scratched her hand and she let him go mid-air. He landed and skulked off into Mary's bedroom. "Sorry, Mother. I sent you a message to tell you I was running late. Did you get it?"

Mary opened her eyes, her pupils bloodshot. She'd been crying. "What message?"

Tara showed her the message on her phone.

I'm running late, I will be there for 7 p.m.

Right beside the reddening scratch on Tara's hand was a red triangle and an exclamation mark on her phone.

Unable to send.

"Oh, Mother, I am so sorry, it never went. I was so busy, I didn't check."

Mary inhaled deeply. "I was so worried, after what happened to me and your father, Lord rest his soul." She blessed herself. "I'm not angry, but all you had to do was check the message sent. Is that too much to ask of my only daughter?"

"No, Mother."

With the food cooked, and on the table, Tara thought she shouldn't let it go to waste. She filled her own plate, then went to take Mary's, but she held her hand out to stop her.

"Not for me, thank you, I've lost my appetite." Mary wiped her forehead like a tortured heroine from an old black and white movie. "How could I possibly eat after what you put me through for the last hour? I thought you were dead. What kept you anyway?"

"It was thirty minutes not an hour and I was talking to a ... a friend." Tara bit into a cold chip. She didn't want to get into anything deep, with Cassie waiting for her and all alone in her apartment, doing God knows what. The plan was to eat, get Mother tucked up in bed and hurry home as soon as possible, but Mother was annoyed and she was like a dog with a bone when she got like this.

"Grace," Mary said.

Tara bowed her head and rushed through the prayer, then picked up another chip.

"You were talking to a friend, were you? And who is she? Is it that Joan from work who has more money than sense?"

"Yes, that's her." It was bad to lie to your mother but sometimes it was the right thing to do. "There's a promotion going in work. It's better money and a higher grade. I'm going to go for it, so I asked Joan for interview advice because she is my supervisor."

"A promotion?" Mary's face drained. "No, no, no. You don't want that. Is it for the money? I could give you more money. A promotion to do what?"

"No, Mother, it's not for money and it's in customer service management. Barry said—"

"Who's Barry?"

"He's my manager and he thinks I'd be good at customer service and management."

Mary tittered, then chuckled, then broke out into a full belly laugh. She banged the table with her fist. "Stop it, you're killing me."

Tara clenched her jaw. "Why is that funny?"

Mary wiped the tears from her eyes, still laughing. "Ah pet, come off it now. Customer service? With people? Sure, that wouldn't suit you at all, you're not a people person. Are you forgetting the first day I brought you to play school?"

Tara hated this story, yet Mother insisted on rolling it out time and again.

"You were the cutest thing with your little pigtails and the pink school bag on your back nearly bigger than you. We didn't even get to the front door before you had a panic attack. I had to bring you home and you refused to go back. You must be the only child ever who quit play school before starting. No, Tara love, I don't think Customer Service would be a good fit for you. Stay away from people and stick with the numbers. You were always good with the numbers."

Tara felt like crying, mostly because her mother was right; she was a terrible people person. What *was* she thinking of going for the job? She was thinking of annoying Joan, that's what ... but couldn't she still do that, if she got the job but didn't take it?

"You're probably right, Mother," she conceded, "but I'll do the interview anyway. It can't hurt."

Mary whipped the plate from under her and stacked it on top of her own. "Remember your father, Lord have mercy on his soul." She blessed herself again and gazed at his framed photo, surrounded by many more, on the wall. "Dear Frank. Worked night and day and it was all taken from him in an instant. I always wondered would he still be with us if we hadn't been arguing about work that Christmas Eve. Promise me you won't take the job."

Tara exhaled. "I promise, Mother."

Mary squeezed her hand. "Good girl. Aren't we grand as we are, me and you? Trucking along like two peas in a pod with no financial worries, but who knows how much time we have left together?"

"Don't say that."

"It's the truth, Tara, and there's no getting around it, but every day we get together is a blessing. I honestly don't know what I'd do without you."

17

CASSIE

Cassie mopped the floor, trying to forget about the bottles of wine in the fridge and how one glass would be enough to settle the nerves – but enough to derail her plans – when she heard the key in the door and rushed to open it.

Tara, weighed down with plastic bags, stood open-mouthed. "You're clean – and this place ... how did you do all this in such a short time?"

Cassie took the bags from her and placed them on the gleaming counter. "I told you I love cleaning, and the time flew. Did you get the cigarettes?"

Tara handed her the pack. "You can smoke on the balcony now; Mother is in bed and her curtains are closed. I have scones and apple tart from Mother's if you're hungry, or would you like something else? I don't cook but I could order takeout for you."

Cassie didn't want food; she wanted a cigarette. "No, the scones will be fine. I'm still a little tender after the lasagne from earlier. I'm going to go out for that smoke."

It was freezing on the wraparound balcony; the cold wind blowing up off the sea would cut you in two, but the sky was clear and full of stars. She shivered as she tried to light the cigarette and got it on the third attempt. The French door opened and Tara joined her.

"Which house is Mary's?" Cassie asked.

Tara gazed across the rooftops. "See the one with the extension and the yellow light?"

The house was mid-terrace, and the extension was long and grey, running into the garden.

"Must be worth some money," Cassie said.

"Yes, I suppose it is, but she'd never sell. She's lived there forever."

Cassie stubbed her cigarette against the wall, put the butt in her box and stood in silence watching the cars pass below. So peaceful, so calm. It felt like home. She'd love Mary's little house; she'd treat it so well if it was hers. She imagined waking up in a bed in her own room in her own house, not worrying about where her next meal would come from, who might come in or about being thrown out. A house was so much more than a roof over her head. It was the stability she'd never had.

"Wow! Did you see that?" Tara asked.

They both looked out into the darkness as a shooting star blazed across the navy sky.

"I did. I wonder if it's a sign. Make a wish."

"I already made my wish and it came true," Tara said. "It's too cold out here, I'm going back inside."

"I'll follow you in."

The apartment was great but there was only one bedroom. If Cassie cleaned and cooked in return for staying on the couch, maybe she could hang out here until Mary

died and then, by right, she'd be entitled to one of the properties. All she had to do was stay sober, stay useful and keep
her mouth shut.

Inside, Tara was on her laptop.

"I'll be with you now; I'm checking the details of an interview I have tomorrow, although I don't think I'll take the job
if I get it."

"Why not?"

"It's probably very stressful and, as Mother pointed out
tonight, I'm not a people person. My boss says I should go
for it, but he doesn't really know me."

Tara looked so pathetic, so beaten, that something stirred
inside Cassie again and, this time, she couldn't bite her
tongue. "I know we just met, hun, and I'm hardly the best
person to give advice, but if your boss recommended you go
for the job, and you want it, then what's stopping you?"

Tara bowed her head, reading whatever was on her
laptop monitor, but Cassie could see she was smiling.

"There's five days' training in the London office," she
read aloud and sighed. "That's the end of that so. Maybe it's
for the best anyway. I wasn't cut out for the job."

Cassie almost kissed her. "Back up there a minute. Why
can't you go to London?"

"Mother needs me here. I couldn't leave her, even if I had
a passport."

Cassie smiled. "A passport is easily sorted and, as for
Mary, consider me your fairy godmother. Cinderella shall go
to the ball because I'm going to help out."

"No, I couldn't possibly ask you to do that – we're practically strangers! I don't know you but what I do know isn't
great. No offence, but I would never leave my dying mother
with someone like you."

Wow – this woman had no filter whatsoever.

"None taken," Cassie said, taking a seat opposite Tara. "When is the training?"

Tara scanned her screen. "It doesn't say."

"It could be after Christmas and maybe we won't be 'practically strangers' by then. Cross that bridge when you come to it, but the offer is there, and remember, whatever I am, she's my mother too."

Tara stopped typing. "Sorry, that was insensitive of me, wasn't it? I didn't mean it to be. I have a habit of annoying people, but I don't do it on purpose. I think it's because I grew up so sheltered. I find it difficult to know what to say and when to say it. Daddy tried to teach me how to be more subtle, but Mother said it was part of my personality and that I was fine as I was. She was, and still is, a great mother. Sorry for the verbal diarrhoea. Sorry."

Cassie jumped up. "Tara, will you stop apologising? I'll put on some coffee."

"I've upset you again." Tara tilted her head. "Oh God, I did. I shouldn't be gushing about how great Mother is when you've never met her."

"It's okay." Cassie continued to the kitchen and switched on the kettle. "I am upset, you're right, but not because of what you said about Mary. You reminded me of a very special lady; the closest thing I ever had to a mother. Mrs Graham. She was very special to me, but ah, it's a long story, you don't want to hear it."

Tara closed her laptop. "I do want to. You've heard so much about me. I want to hear about you and I'm not only saying it because it's the right thing to do."

Cassie then told Tara all about the kindest woman she'd ever met.

FROM THE MOMENT she set foot on the white carpet in Margaret Graham's beautiful home, five-year-old Cassie had felt like a fish out of water.

Set on rolling green fields looking over the ocean, the white-washed bungalow with roses growing up the garden walls was like a fairy-tale castle to Cassie compared to the grey walls of Cherish the Child.

"You are very welcome to our home," Mrs Graham told her as she showed her to her room. Pink, floral and lacy, dolls and teddys scattered on her bed. Against the far wall stood a filled bookcase and the large woman opened the wardrobe to reveal the most beautiful clothes Cassie had ever seen. Dresses hanging in every colour and little shoes laid neatly beside each other.

"Thank you," Cassie said politely, but when she spotted the baby doll, the tears came.

Mrs Graham pulled her to her ample bosom and wrapped her in a tight hug. "Ah, pet, I know. You've been through the mill, haven't you?"

She pulled back, her kind eyes full of tears as she held Cassie's hands. "This is your home now; you are part of our family."

"Thank you," Cassie repeated.

Mrs Graham chuckled and sighed. "Ah, it's a big change for us all but a good change. I'll let you settle in while I get dinner ready and then you can meet the rest of the family. Give me those dirty clothes and I'll run them through the wash for you."

Cassie couldn't speak in the face of such kindness. Mrs Graham hunkered down to Cassie's level. "Tell you what, pet, you get settled and when you're ready you can come to us, okay, sweetie?"

The woman left, closing the white painted door behind her and Cassie inhaled the scent of her own coat. She liked Mrs Graham but didn't want to give her clothes to her. If they were washed, the smell would be gone. Fully clothed, shoes and all, she took the baby doll and climbed up onto the white wrought-iron bed, which squeaked as she snuggled under the pink floral quilt and fell fast asleep.

When she woke up, her face was warm and the room was a dull orange as the winter sun set. She stretched out, much calmer and more rested than when she'd arrived.

"That's my doll."

Cassie jumped up to see an older black-haired girl holding a tiny black kitten and standing at the foot of her bed. She pulled herself up quickly and brushed her hair back from her face.

"I'm Cassie," she said. "Is that your kitten? What's its name?"

The girl looked her up and down and her eyes landed on the doll in the bed. "I know who you are. My God, you're a show, even worse than I expected. Mammy said you have to get dressed and come up for dinner, and don't even think about calling her Mammy, she's not your Mammy and she never will be your Mammy. She's my Mammy, okay? Now, give me Daisy and get changed into something that doesn't stink or Daddy will flip." She swiped the baby doll from Cassie and flounced out of the room, kitten and all.

Cassie held back the tears and pulled on a woollen dress that was hanging in the wardrobe, then followed the chatter up the hall and into the living room, where a large balding man and the black-haired girl sat along with Mrs Graham.

On seeing her, Mrs Graham jumped up. "Loveen, come in. Here, sit here." She pulled out a chair opposite the girl, who narrowed her eyes at Cassie as she took her place in front of a large bowl of stew. A plate of buttered bread sat on the table.

"Don't make a fuss of her, dear," the man said and, looking over his glasses, offered his hand. "Dessie Graham, pleased to meet you. And you are?"

"Cassie Blake, Mister, pleased to meet you too," she said and gave him a smile, a smile that wasn't returned.

"She needs a bath after dinner," he told his wife and the black-haired girl grinned.

"Enough chat, food's getting cold," Mrs Graham said. Cassie had never seen so much food. She tried a potato and then a carrot. Delicious, and so she took a piece of bread and got stuck in with gusto.

"This is Kimberley, our daughter, and Fluffy her new kitten," Mrs Graham told Cassie. "We thought it might be nice for her to have a sister, isn't that right, Kim? Someone to play with."

Kimberley tutted and muttered under her breath. "*You* thought it might be nice, you mean. I already have Fluffy to play with."

"Now, now, we talked about this. Be nice," Mrs Graham said.

All through the meal, Mr Graham quizzed Cassie about her life and the home and then freaked out when she said she'd never been to school.

"Oh, we'll have to get that rectified right away," Mr Graham said. "Our Kimberley is a straight A student, and she plays fabulous piano. You have a long way to come."

Kimberley gasped too. "No school? Oh my God, what sort of a vagabond are you?"

Cassie was beginning to feel sick. She wasn't used to eating so much food in one go and now her tummy was gurgling. "I don't feel good—"

"Now, Kimberley," Mr Graham said, ignoring Cassie's pleas, "remember your mother wanted this, and we agreed to give her a chance."

A bead of sweat trickled down Cassie's back and her gut contracted. She stood to go to the bathroom.

"Sit down," Mr Graham demanded. "We do not leave the table until we are finished eating. We have manners in this house and do not interrupt conversation. My, my, we have our work cut out with you, don't we? It seems school is only the tip of the iceberg."

"Do you need the toilet, love?" Mrs Graham asked in a kind voice.

Cassie nodded.

"Well, then you are excused," she said.

Cassie tried to stand again, but she felt horribly dizzy and then, suddenly, it was too late. Her violent spew hit Kimberley right in the face, covering her clothes, her hair and the little black kitten, who leapt from her arms. She screamed and Cassie ran from the table, spewing as she went, all over the white carpet all the way down to the bathroom.

"Daaaaddeeeeecy!" she heard Kimberley wail in a flurry of frantic activity. "Send her back. I don't want a sister and I don't want her. I hate her."

A door slammed shut and Cassie cried for Ireland. She'd really blown it.

They didn't send her back, not straight away anyway. Mrs

Graham said everyone deserved a second chance. They let her get used to school and a warm safe bed and good food. They let her have hope, but after six months of hell Mrs Graham gave up.

She carried Cassie's black sack up the big hill to the home, crying every step of the way. "This is not your fault, pet. You're a good girl and you've a kind soul. If I could keep you I would, you know that, don't you?"

Cassie felt numb and almost relieved. No more daily hatred from Kimberley and Mr Graham treating her like dirt, but she would miss Mrs Graham, who had been nothing but kind to her and had insisted she continue attending school, which the home had agreed to.

"Will you come visit me?" Cassie asked, and Mrs Graham pondered for a moment before answering.

"Yes. Yes, I will. I will visit you every week, but we must keep it our little secret, okay? We won't tell Kimberley or Old Mr Grumpy." She held out her warm hand for Cassie to shake. "Deal?"

Cassie giggled. "Deal."

At the gates, Mrs Graham rang the bell and Sister Agnes came out to meet them. Mrs Graham pulled her into the softest, warmest hug and together they cried. Then Cassie took her black sack and went through the gates and into the massive grey building. She had nothing left of her time with the Grahams but memories and Daisy, the doll she'd stolen, in her case.

She was back in the place that would be her home until she left at the age of sixteen.

18

___

TARA

Friday, 11 November

Tara woke on the couch to the sound of bacon sizzling in the pan. The room was dark except for the dim aura coming from the spotlights over the kitchen cupboards where Cassie cooked. She must have fallen asleep while they chatted.

She snuggled under the warm duvet while Cassie put bacon on a plate and carried it past her to the dining table. The pyjamas were so big on her she looked like a little girl and, as she leaned over to put the plates on the table, the sunlight shone through, revealing a silhouette of a tiny waist and long, slim legs. Cassie swung around and caught her looking.

"Ah, good morning sleepy head. I was about to call you, big day ahead!"

"Good morning," Tara said and stretched out. "What time is it?"

"Almost seven, plenty of time yet. I hope you don't mind me taking liberties, but I went ahead with the breakfast and cleaned up the dishes from last night."

"Not at all, thank you! Wait, what time did you wake up at and where did you sleep?"

Cassie returned to the kitchen and fetched a coffee pot that Tara didn't even know she had.

"Oh, I was grand; pulled a few chairs together. I don't really sleep," Cassie replied. "I'm more of a napper. Probably all the years of watching my back in and out of dodgy places, you know? Come on up to the table and get started. Will you have an egg? I'll make you an egg, how do you like it?"

Tara dragged herself from her warm makeshift bed and sat up to the table. She yawned, so tired that her vision was blurry, but still, she could make out the feast in front of her. Sausages, rashers, toast and coffee. She put some on her plate and poured the coffee, wishing she could stay there all day, but the traffic building outside reminded her of all the things she had to do. "No egg for me, thanks," she called to Cassie, who was now frying something on a pan Tara had never used. "I've more than enough here, come sit down yourself."

Cassie flipped an egg onto a plate and joined Tara at the table. She piled the egg and two bacon rashers onto a slice of buttered toast then lashed them with ketchup and completed the sandwich with a second slice of toast. She bit in. "Aw, man, this is delicious. Thank you."

"Thank yourself, you made it," Tara replied with a smile.

"No, I mean thank you for everything. Last night was a dream come true for me."

Tara yawned. "It was nice for me too. I get the train at 8 a.m., so will you make sure you're ready?"

Cassie stood and began to clear the table. "I thought we got on well and you liked me being around."

"We do, Cassie. Having you cook and clean is nice, very nice, but you're a homeless alcoholic I met two days ago, and I can't pretend you're not. No, it's better that you leave. If I let you stay it's called enabling. That's what the counsellor said who came to talk to us at work. It's far kinder if I let you stand on your own two feet, plus you did rob my wallet, so I can't trust you in the apartment on your own. That's the truth."

Cassie looked like she'd been kicked in the stomach. "Say what you feel, Tara, no seriously, don't sugar coat it for my benefit. I'm not a stranger, we have proof, DNA proof, that we are sisters and I didn't even know I'd robbed you, and when I realised I returned the wallet, didn't I?"

She had a point. "I suppose."

Cassie's eyes narrowed. "Do you know what? Don't bother your head, we're never going to make it past that night. I thought that I could help you; give you space to live a little, get that job, travel, but I know where I'm not wanted. I'll go with you on the train and go back to Mayo. We might cross paths again in the future sometime, that's if I don't get raped or die in the meantime choking on my own vomit. I'll get ready to go."

Cassie stomped off and Tara followed her. "That's not fair. You said one night, and I let you stay one night. I don't want you to die, but I don't know you. You have to understand that!"

Cassie inhaled deeply. "Of course I understand and you're right, a deal is a deal. I asked for one night and you gave me one night. I'll be on my way and we can meet again sometime. Now, you have an important interview today and have to look your best. I've left fresh towels in the bathroom. Bring your clothes out to me and I'll iron them while you're in there."

Cassie followed Tara to her room but waited at the door. "Don't worry, I didn't go into your room. I didn't want to overstep any boundaries."

Tara picked her new dress up off the floor and held it out to Cassie. "I appreciate it."

Cassie swiped it from her. "Yeah, whatever."

In the shower, Tara's stomach hurt. She felt bad that Mother and Daddy RIP had abandoned Cassie, but if they'd known she was having such a hard life they would have taken her back home. She was sure of that. But there was something else bugging her, something new that she couldn't put her finger on.

Back out in the messy room, Tara put on the freshly pressed dress that lay on her bed. Her new outfit would come in handy, after all. Cassie passed by with the folded ironing board that Mother had bought for her but which had never been used. Until now.

"You look great. That's a nice dress. Is it a bit big on you?"

"It's the one I wore when we met and no, it's the way I want it."

Cassie stopped. "I'm sorry. I should mind my own business and I'm sorry about our first meeting. I don't know why I drank so much; it was so important to me to meet you. I wish I could turn back time and make a better first impression, but I can't."

That feeling twinged again in Tara's stomach and she examined her thoughts to find what it was. Should she say thanks for breakfast? No, she already did that. She let her stay for a night, as agreed. Unless ... "Cassie, I was thinking about you going this morning."

Cassie's eyes lit up. "Yeah?"

"It's not right to make you leave with nowhere to go. Take your time here today, find somewhere to stay and pull the door when you leave this afternoon, but please don't drink and don't rob anything."

Cassie threw her arms around her. "Thank you, thank you, thank you. I'm so grateful and to show you I am going to gut this place, make it sparkle."

Tara hugged her back, which was not weird at all but nice. "Okay, but you can relax too. See if you can find a place to stay." She opened the drawers in the kitchen cabinet and pulled out table mats, cloths, cards, sponges and a mobile phone, which she plugged into her charger beside the cooker.

"You can use this, it's my work phone. The code is 4321. See if you can find somewhere to stay. Don't answer it unless it's me."

"Thank you, not just for the phone and letting me stay, but for letting me into your life. I know this is early stages for us both, but I feel a real connection with you, like sisters should. Am I right or am I imagining it?"

Tara's stomach settled. "No, you're right. I feel it too."

Cassie stopped scrubbing the dishes and turned, her eyes wet. "Tara, I'd like to meet her. I'd like to meet Mary."

Tara gasped. "Mother? Oh no, I don't think so."

"I won't tell her who I am. I'll pretend I'm your friend."

"No way! I've never brought anyone to meet her."

There were never any callers growing up. Mother would go out for groceries and banking, stuff she needed to do, but then the accident happened, and the only people Mary saw now were Tara and her doctor.

Cassie's lip wobbled. "It's that – no, it doesn't matter, you've been very good to me."

"What is it?"

"Do you not think I've waited long enough?" She set down the cloth. "You know, to meet my mother?"

19

CASSIE

Cassie lay on the couch, grinning from ear to ear. Not only had she met her sister, she had found somewhere to stay with huge long-term potential. She snuggled into Tara's shape, still moulded into the cushions, and pulled the duvet over her. This was an incredible outcome; the repercussions made her as giddy as the prospect of staying sober made her anxious. She closed her eyes.

In the cornfield, she cradled her grazed knees. The vines of the corn plants wrapped around her bare legs and beeped. Beeped?

Cassie gasped awake, covered in sweat, her heart pounding in her chest when another beep sounded. It was coming from the kitchen.

The phone! She jumped up to the counter to find two WhatsApp messages, both from Tara.

I asked Mother. She said you can come for dinner tonight.

I'll come by for you after work.

Cassie's heart skipped. She replied.

Really, hun? I can see her? TYSM!

Cassie had to sit down. She was going to meet Mary, the woman who was pretending to be Tara's mother. Did she pay for her? Of course, she did. There was nothing money couldn't buy. The phone beeped again. Tara.

I told her you are my friend Joan from work. I'll explain when I get home, have to go to this interview now. Dinner's at 6:30 p.m.

Cassie replied.

Best of luck with the interview, hun. I'll be ready.

The phone display said it was 8:57 a.m. Not even nine o'clock. The whole day stretched in front of her and the sudden urge to drink almost overwhelmed her. She opened the fridge and stared at the two wine bottles. Her heartbeat increased.

Take a breather and use your head.

A cigarette would do but she couldn't go out to the balcony in case Mary saw her and Tara hadn't left a key for the apartment. The walls started to spin, and she watched herself open the fridge door and pour wine into a glass.

Decide, don't react.

She put the glass on the counter and paced the living

room, trying to think but she couldn't. Returning to the glass, she swirled it, smelled it, felt it, then emptied it down the sink as quick as she could, followed by the remaining contents of the two bottles in the fridge. Out of breath and with adrenaline coursing through her veins, she searched through every kitchen press for more bottles and, when she was sure there was none, broke down in tears on the kitchen floor.

It still wasn't even close to midday. She'd clean the windows. In the broom cupboard at the end of the hall, she took out the extendable window cleaner, still in its wrapper. Beside it was a glossy gift bag and inside a bottle of red staring back at her. She had to get out of here and quick. Throwing on her runners, she grabbed her coat and cigarettes and was out of the apartment within seconds, the lack of a key least of her worries. Taking a few deep breaths, she put the door on the latch and hoped nobody would try their luck today.

Outside, she inhaled deeply. She'd only meant to put some space between the wine and herself, but out here gulls squawked overhead and boats bobbed on the calm water of the harbour. Blue bollards glistened against the yellow sand and soon she found herself on the promenade, joining walkers and their dogs and putting one foot in front of the other. Then another and another.

This was exactly what she needed, to feel part of something bigger. Cassie walked and walked – all the way to Portmarnock and back again. The time passed in clumps – going slowly in places then whizzing by. It was after lunchtime when Cassie finally felt hungry again and longed for a few euro to buy a chicken fillet roll from the Spar shop. Passing a pub, the dim lights, gentle clink of glasses and soft chatter called to her. The door swung open and a red-faced punter spilled out, the warm air beckoning her inside.

Come on in. It's safe here, you're one of us. No trying or distraction needed in here. Come on, you know you'll be back sooner or later. Why suffer?

She closed her eyes and inhaled the hops hanging in the air as Sharon's words echoed in her head.

Think of something to aim for. Something to stay clean for.

"I have nothing and nobody," Cassie had said.

Oh, but you do. You have so much, if you opened your eyes to see.

No, she was meeting Mary today. After all these years, she would be face to face with the woman who raised her sister. There was too much at stake to throw it away over one poxy drink. She pulled up her hood and walked on by. Outside the apartment complex, she lit up her last cigarette with no memory of smoking half of them. Mary's house was straight ahead as the crow flew but obscured from view behind guesthouse after guesthouse.

She could pretend to be Joan. Hell, she could be Mother Teresa if that's what it took. All she had to do was stay sober, bite her tongue and bide her time. Nobody else knew the truth. Then this walk, this town, this life could be hers. Finally, something to stay clean for.

She punched in the codes that she'd deduced from the pattern of Tara's fingers last night and entered the complex and the apartment building. A man passed her in the lobby and stared. She kept her head down and called the lift, which came immediately, and she watched him leave the building. She would have to do something with herself if she wanted to stay here without drawing attention.

20

TARA

It was strange getting on the train glammed up and with a cooked breakfast inside her. Tara yawned in the morning sunshine on the unusually quiet platform. Although exhausted, she couldn't stop smiling. Her sister was in her apartment and the icing on the cake for the day so far was when the train arrived on time with many empty seats.

The night before was magic. Her smile widened as she realised – it was a sleepover. She'd never had a friend, and certainly never one who stayed over before. All those books she read as a lonely teenager, all the Hollywood movies that made her cry, they described sleepovers as the best fun a girl could have.

Cassie wanted to meet Mother. She said she wouldn't tell her the truth about who she was, and Tara believed her, but that wasn't the issue. Bringing anybody into her house would stress her mother out.

Tara cried the day Mother got her prognosis, especially

because she should have been there to support her but had instead been in bed with a hangover. Oh, how she wished she hadn't gone to the Partners Plus summer party. That had been a bad, bad decision.

Her mother was never exactly outgoing, but after Daddy RIP died it was like the house had been ripped apart. It took a long time to shrink the massive holes he left, the pipe he left on the fireplace, the newspaper left open on the horseracing, the remote controls always stuck down the side of his old brown armchair. To this day, she never sat in Daddy's Chair. Nobody did. When he passed, a bit of both of them died too. He was the jolly one, and she used to wonder how he'd married someone as introverted as her mother, but he worshipped the ground she walked on, idolised her. "My Mary," he'd say, "made me the happiest man in the world." He'd pull her from whatever she was teaching Tara and waltz her around the room. She'd smack him playfully and then let him lead her, throwing her head back and laughing. Then he'd pick up Tara and together the trio would dance, like a very happy family.

There was no sign of Barry on the train this morning, which disappointed her a little. She didn't fancy him with his funny eyebrows and fat neck, but she felt better when he was around. Trains ran every few minutes at rush hour, he could be on any one of them, or driving his car if it had made a miraculous recovery. Maybe he'd bought a new one already. She wondered if he was thinking about her too.

She messaged her mother.

> Can I bring my friend to dinner tonight?

Two ticks.

Mother typing.

A dinner guest? Is it a boyfriend?

Unlikely. She'd never had a boyfriend, but then she never had a friend either.

No. It's Joan from work.

Mother typing ... Pause ... Mother typing.

Lovely. Usual time? What will she eat?

That was easier than she'd thought.

Thanks, Mother. I don't know what she likes, I'm sure she will love whatever you cook. See you then.

She messaged Cassie to tell her and Cassie replied almost instantly. In time, maybe they would tell her mother the truth, but she couldn't risk giving her such a big shock, nor could she face the subsequent fallout from that. Besides, she wasn't sure how long Cassie would be around. No, this would do for now; it was more than enough.

In the office, she made coffee in a disposable cup and brought it to her desk. Joan stomped by and tutted, but nothing was going to bring Tara down today. A few of her colleagues did a double take when they saw her, but then went back to their work. Tara switched on her PC – the difference a flowery dress made was stupid. With an hour to go until the interview, she set about running off reports for this afternoon's team meeting and downloaded a document from Google: *Common Interview Questions.*

At 9:57 a.m., she took the lift to the fourth floor.

The lift doors opened to another world. For a start, there was carpet. Glass walls and a glass door separated the corridor from the Partners Plus offices. A huge metallic sign hung on the wall behind the receptionist, who had white funky hair and a huge, veneered smile. Tara rapped on the glass and she buzzed her in.

"Tara Ryan interviewing for customer liaison team lead," Tara said.

"Ah, yes. Hi, Tara, I'll let them know you're here," the receptionist said, with a wave to indicate she should take a seat in the decorated waiting area.

It was like an ice palace and obviously a professional interior-design job. So much going on, yet so subtle and tasteful, unlike the tacky and tired decorations on the ground floor. It was a winter wonderland here ... even the massive Christmas tree was white, with every decoration glass.

Tara sat in the black leather armchair that was oh so comfortable and picked up the *Financial Times*, pretending to read it. The morning sun streamed through the window and hit her eyes hard, the words dancing on the pages. She blocked out the sun with her hand and focused on the white tree instead. Thankfully the lights were not switched on – that's if it had any. She couldn't risk a migraine today.

"Hey, Tara, glad you came. We're ready for you now." It was Barry in white shirt and black trousers. He guided her through the plush fourth floor and to the meeting room at the end of the corridor. "Any change of mind on my birthday drinks tomorrow night? It would be great if you could come. Also, Leo Harris is here. I didn't know, he joined us last minute. I'm sorry if this makes you uncomfortable."

Tara didn't have time to formulate a reply as they arrived at the room, its door open. Inside people chatted around a huge mahogany table.

"Heather, Matt, this is Tara," Barry said.

A woman and man offered their hands and Tara shook them.

"I know you've met Leo before," Barry said. "He insisted on being here."

The tall, grey-haired man leaned back on his chair at the top of the table. "You don't mind if I sit in on the meeting, do you, Tara?" he said. A shiver ran through her. She hated how he pronounced her name. Tora.

"No," she said and accepted the seat beside Barry.

"I've been telling Matt what a good worker you are," Barry said. "He thinks you will make a great asset to their team up here on the fourth floor and Heather is from HR."

Tara's collar felt tight.

"Hi, Tara," Heather from HR said. "Don't mind me, I'm only here to observe. Pretend I'm not even in the room." She swatted away an invisible fly.

Matt sat back in his chair and twirled his pen. "So, what do you need to know? The role is with the customer care team; it's an immediate start, comes with full training, a salary increase of ten per cent and an extra two days holiday per annum. How does that sound?"

This was weird. No *where do you want to be in five years?* questions like she expected. Those questions were stupid anyway.

"Excuse me," she said. "To be clear, are you offering me the job now?"

Matt smiled and fixed his tie. "Yes. Yes, we are. What do you say, Tara?"

"Thank you."

He laughed. "I mean, Tara, do you want the job?"

"Oh, sorry. Can I think about it?"

"Don't take too long," Leo Harris said. He hadn't taken his eyes off her. The last time he looked at her like that ... well, she didn't want to think about it.

Matt clapped his hands. "Oh, I almost forgot. The training is in the London office, starting the second week in December. I know it's soon, but better have it over with before Christmas, ready to hit the ground running in the new year. I assume that won't be a problem."

"I'm going too, with the latest recruits," Barry said. "You won't be going alone."

"Second week in December?" Tara asked. "I didn't know it would be so soon."

"Best to get on with it, don't you think? Organise with Jason in travel on second as soon as possible. He'll get you into the same hotel as the others."

Travel. How lovely that would be, her first time on an aeroplane, but it was impossible. "I'm sorry, I can't. I care for my elderly mother and there is nobody else to help."

Leo Harris stood, towering over her. "I'll tell you what, *Tora*. Take the weekend to decide. Go home and see if you can work something out for your mother. Will you do that, like a good girl? Now, let's get you back to work."

He led her back through the office with his hand on her lower back; a man used to getting what he wanted. A man with no idea what real responsibility, or caring, was. A man who got lucky when Tara dropped the charges.

"Mr Harris, about this training, I don't think—"

"Megan, can you send in David Farrell, please?" He was talking to himself – no, to his earpiece. "Well done, Tora. Good job."

Well done, Tora. Good job. Tara shuddered.

C assie pushed the unlocked door of Tara's apartment and let herself back in, then switched on the TV, where the 4 p.m. news had started.

Today, in the latest on the Cherish the Child home scandal, survivors descend on Government Buildings, demanding all remaining records. Survivor Anne Murray spoke to us exclusively.

"Denny was my baby brother," a middle-aged woman with white hair and glasses said. *"He was in the nursery and I was in the orphanage. One day he disappeared and nobody would tell me what happened to him."*

She broke down. *"I never saw him again. I don't know if he died or was sold. Please tell me what happened to him. It's cruel to leave me like this. I just want answers."*

Cassie couldn't watch any more. How had such evil been allowed to happen in this country? Money, that's how. Money, babies and desperate women like Mary willing to buy them, no questions asked. She switched off the TV and made coffee, adding the last few drops of milk from the carton, then texted Tara to pick up more milk on her way home. Curling up on the sofa, she gazed out at the dark sea, exhausted but exhilarated. Those chairs were impossible to sleep on last night and, when she was still twisting and turning at 5 a.m., she'd got up to make a start on breakfast. But she was lucky. She'd found her sister. She'd found Tara.

Cassie couldn't remember Tara's name before she was taken. Maybe she had no name at all. Did Mary name her or was that Them? It suited her; she looked like a Tara.

Be useful. Doing things for others will benefit you too. The more you get out of your head, the better you will feel and the more valuable you will be to yourself and to others.

She yawned. The adrenaline from earlier had left her body, leaving her shattered. Still, though, she hadn't had any alcohol and that was incredible. Starting to drift, she caught herself and jumped up. The day was getting on and Tara would be home in a few hours, so she shook herself and set about giving the bathrooms a deep clean. The mop and bucket were in the cupboard at the end of the hall and so was the bottle of wine. She took a deep breath – she could do this. As she passed Tara's room, her attention was drawn to the mess. It was like a bomb hit it. How could one person cause so much destruction? She paused for a moment outside the door but couldn't help herself going in. She stripped the bed, taking the sheets and the clothes scattered around the room to the washing machine. While putting them on for a cycle, she stripped off and threw her own in too.

The washer and dryer warmed the open-plan apartment, the sound of industry calming her spirit. When the laundry was dried and folded, she took the warm, fresh piles to the bedroom and laid them out. Opening the wardrobe, she was astonished to find it almost bare. Not very much for a whole life, about the same as she had in her black holdall, although more than she had now.

Including Tara's laundry, there was six of everything – skirts, jumpers, shirts and leggings. The underwear was the same – six knickers, six bras and six pairs of socks. One outfit for every day, Cassie reckoned, the seventh being worn today.

She put the sheets, towels and pillowcases away, then wiped down Tara's bedside locker, where a framed photograph sat of Tara and an old woman in a wheelchair. Mary. The dying woman.

The lying woman.

A clear blue document folder jutted out from the shelf beneath. She pulled it out to see a label with "Personal Documents" on it. If she had a little peek, Tara would never know. She sat on the bed and looked through the documents – Tara's bank details, tax details and a birth cert.

A birth cert for Tara Ryan, whose mother was Mary Ryan, a homemaker and formerly a teacher, and whose father was Frank Ryan, a teacher.

She wanted to cry. It wasn't fair, but feeling sorry for herself wouldn't help. She put the documents back in the folder and left it exactly where she found it.

Back in the living room, Cassie made yet another mug of instant coffee, this time black. She sat at the table just out of sight of the window in the dark, just in case Mary looked up and saw the curtains closed or, worse, Cassie in the apartment. It was completely dark outside, except for the lights from the traffic and houses around. How much did this place actually cost? A quick google of properties in Cushla confirmed it – €600k. That seemed ridiculously expensive for a one-bed apartment to Cassie, but she was hardly qualified to make that assumption. She wasn't qualified at anything, having left school as early as she could. She'd done courses and gone on training programmes, but being tied to a schedule suffocated her and made her want to rebel more. The only jobs she ever stayed in were caring and cleaning. She was happiest doing those until the rumours started again and she was sacked.

When the key turned in the front door, she jumped, knocking the coffee over the glass table. It dripped on her newly cleaned black jeans and the wooden floor. She rushed to the kitchen to get a cloth as Tara entered in slow motion, her head down and her hair messy. Her face was like a bulldog chewing a wasp as she threw her backpack on the counter, her eyes fixed on the empty washing machine and only then did she acknowledge Cassie. "You did my washing?"

She was like a different woman than the one who left this morning.

Cassie's anxiety flew into overdrive. "I hope you don't mind. I took the liberty of giving the place a deep clean. I needed to keep busy."

Tara closed the curtains and switched on the lights, all the while muttering to herself, then she cocked her head at Cassie. "I see you washed your clothes too."

She brushed down her freshly laundered top. "Yes, I hope that's okay. If I am to stay here, I can't look shabby, can I? Plus, I thought if I'm supposed to be your friend Joan from work, I should look respectable."

Tara's face contorted. "Joan is *not* my friend. I told Mother that to keep her happy." Her eyes dropped and she continued to talk, almost to herself. "She broke my best mug on purpose. She didn't even apologise. Good girl.

That's what he said *good girl* and now I can't go. London. Can't go."

"Tara. Are you okay? What happened to you?"

Her eyes were dead and she continued to mutter. "Doesn't matter. Another thing I can't do. Ah well, who cares? Nobody. It is what it is. We have to be grateful for every day. Every day is a blessing."

Cassie held her by the shoulders. "Tara, stop. Something has upset you. What happened?"

"I'll change for dinner; we have to leave soon," Tara said and opened the fridge, then stopped. "Where's the wine?"

"I threw it out. I should have asked but I was so close to drinking it, it had to go."

Tara narrowed her eyes. "Don't lie to me. Don't make a fool of me."

"I'm not lying to you," Cassie said, trailing Tara to her bedroom. "I hope you don't mind but I—"

Tara stood at the doorway, facing her spotless bedroom. "You cleaned my room."

"I did, but I didn't drink. I poured it out, I swear."

"You cleaned my room," Tara repeated.

"I know you told me not to, but I couldn't leave the apartment and, with the temptation of the alcohol, I needed to keep busy. It was a joy for me, a way to work through my emotions. I didn't mind."

Tara's eyes darted to the pine chest of drawers with the photo on top. "What did you touch?"

The blue folder seemed to stick out further than this morning. "Tara, I didn't open your drawers, I swear. I cleaned what was in plain sight, that's all."

She hadn't opened the drawers, that was the truth.

"I told you not to come in here and you didn't listen. It's

like I'm invisible in my own life. You're the same as everyone else. You need to leave."

———

THEY WALKED the short distance in silence and stopped at the garden gate of a small, terraced house. Sandwiched between one on the left and two on the right, it would barely fetch €80k in Mayo, but this was Cushla and was valued at €750k. Tara was still raging like nothing Cassie had ever seen, huffing and puffing like a child.

She'd blown it. She was full sure Tara would want her to stay when she saw how valuable she was but instead she'd gone too far. Let herself down again. Acted first, thought later.

Tara opened the garden gate. "Mother thinks you are Joan, my friend from work. You had DNA test results that said your cousin was your boyfriend and you broke up. I never told her where you're from, and she's going to know your accent, so you can say you're from somewhere west. Mother is old but she is bright so don't volunteer any information. I told her I went for drinks with Joan the night I met you. That's all you need to know. Oh, and she's dying so don't upset her."

Cassie took a deep breath. "Tara, I am sorry. I shouldn't have done what I did, but I swear to you I didn't drink."

"No, you shouldn't." Tara continued up the path.

With the sudden realisation she was about to come face to face with Mary, Cassie's legs stopped moving. Frozen to the spot, she gasped. "Can you give me a moment? This is big."

Tara's face softened, a flicker of recognition, like tuning

in a channel, and then she was back to this morning's version of herself. "Yes. Of course. It's your first time meeting Mother, I forgot. Sorry."

Cassie leaned against the hedge and took deep breaths. "I didn't think I would be this nervous."

"You'll be fine, she's lovely – unless we're late." Tara turned the key and opened the door, leaving Cassie with no option but to follow her in.

The heat and smell of cooking mixed with cat litter rushed out, turning Cassie's stomach.

"Mother, we're here," Tara called.

A tiny elderly woman in a wheelchair came out to meet them. "Hello," she said, her accent achingly familiar. "Joan, you're welcome. I've heard all about you. I'm Mary."

It was almost too much standing in front of this woman. Cassie focused on keeping calm, and thankfully Mary diverted her attention to Tara, allowing her to catch her breath.

"Oh, why the face, love?" Mary asked. "Did the interview not go well?"

The interview! Cassie had forgotten all about it.

"There's nothing wrong, I'm tired that's all, and actually the interview went very well. I got the job."

"Good girl," Mary said. "Congratulations, but you're not taking it, sure you're not?"

Tara flushed. "No, I'm not taking it."

Cassie wanted to ask why, but after the debacle earlier she let it go. "Something smells amazing," she said, ignoring the white cat eyeballing her while relieving itself into a litter tray.

"It's a simple beef stroganoff," Mary said. "Tara's not too

keen but she needs her iron. Anaemic, she is, gets very run down, the poor thing."

Cassie was anaemic too, always was, but she didn't volunteer that information.

"Come in, both of you, and sit down while I bring in the food." Mary led them into a living room straight from the 1980s. Old, quaint, dated, charming. Like Cassie imagined it would be, except for the stench that the other women seemed oblivious to.

Cassie followed Mary into the kitchen. "I'll give you a hand."

"You'll do no such thing. I'm well able."

Tara threw Cassie a look. "She likes to be independent, so let her."

Mary brought the food, bowl by bowl, while Tara sat there like a big child. The walls were covered in framed family photographs and a mahogany table filled the end of the elongated room.

Cassie swallowed a lump. She hadn't even one picture of her childhood yet there were so many of Tara. In the centre was a wedding picture of a much younger couple. Mary and Frank. They looked so happy.

"That's Daddy RIP," Tara whispered. "He was amazing, you would have loved him. I'm sorry for being angry at you earlier. Daddy wouldn't like me being like this. He liked me being happy."

A plate hit the carpet behind them. Cassie rushed to pick it up. "That's the end of it, Mary. I know you are well able, but I insist on helping."

"Nonsense, you two will want to be chatting. Sit yourself down there and let me look after my guests."

Mary returned to the kitchen and Tara sobbed. "I miss

him so much." Cassie reached for her hand and she let her take it. She gave it a squeeze, then dropped it when she heard Mary returning.

After saying Grace, which Cassie knew like the back of her hand from the nuns, along with what seemed like every prayer that was ever written, they tucked in. The food was delicious, but it was hard to eat, knowing what she knew. For the rest of the meal, Mary played with her food, swirling it around her plate and asking questions.

"Where are you from yourself, Joan?" Mary asked.

"Galway." Close enough.

"Ah the West, a great part of the country. I'm from there myself, Mayo. Though I've been gone a very long time now. Have you family?"

Cassie coughed. "Sorry?"

"Family? Have you a husband or children, a family?"

"No family," she said.

Mary smiled. "Ah, a career woman, although I suppose women can have it all nowadays – work, family, social life, the lot. It was different in my time." She gazed into the distance. "I was a teacher, you know. I was good at my job, but back then women had to give up working when they got married to make room for men, to support their families, plus children needed their mother. The marriage ban it was called; did you hear of it?"

"I didn't," Cassie replied. "That doesn't seem fair."

"It was the way it was. If you were a civil servant like me, you had to give it all up, no questions asked. I remember my mother telling me about it when I was applying for teaching college, and I was angry. I challenged her, asking why I should bother when all I was going to be was a skivvy when I got married."

She turned to Cassie. "Everyone got married then, and young too. Well, she clipped me 'round the ear and told me that was exactly why I needed to work hard. A well-educated woman, she said, was an attractive proposition to a successful man as both a wife and mother to his future children. She said he would provide for me, and in return I would serve him. So, no, Joan, it wasn't a bit fair, but she was right too. Frank did provide for us. Before and after he died."

Mary blessed herself and looked at the wedding photo on the wall of that fine-looking couple, both so happy, and so young.

"He was a handsome man," Cassie said. "What was he like?"

"Frank? He was a good man – conservative, some may say boring, but a good man. That picture was taken straight after our wedding ceremony, we were so happy. Oh, we did it differently in those days, a small affair with a few friends and family, none of these three-day events they have today." Mary had a glint in her eye. "We went off on honeymoon that very evening, sure we were mad to do it."

"Mother! I don't want to hear that," Tara exclaimed, which made Cassie laugh.

Mary continued despite Tara's protests. "I know the young crowd don't put any value on celibacy these days, but we'd saved ourselves for marriage. It was a no-brainer for people of our profession; Frank was a teacher too. Pregnancy out of wedlock was a huge scandal and was too big a risk for us both. There was no contraception back then. Then we got married and Tara came along; she was worth the wait."

Decide don't react. Decide don't react.

"Mother, please! Less of your love life, I'm eating," Tara

said and Mary winked at Cassie. "We more than made up for waiting, let me tell you."

At the end of the evening, Mary showed them out to the hall. "Joan, that was the best evening I've had in a very long time. Thank you so much for coming."

"Not at all, Mary, the pleasure was all mine. You're very good for having me and the dinner was gorgeous."

"Anytime. We had a wonderful night, didn't we, Tara?"

Tara opened the front door. "We did."

"You're very welcome to come again, Joan," Mary called, as they walked down the garden path. "Would you come tomorrow? Ah, forget it, that's stupid, you've probably got plans."

Cassie stopped and turned around. "I'd love to, Mary, but it's not up to me."

Tara hesitated. "Not tomorrow night. I have a work party."

"Sure, then wouldn't Joan be going with you?" Mary said. "I'll tell you what. I'll cook an early dinner and you can both go out after that. Say 6 p.m., how does that sound?"

"Fiiine," Tara said. "We'll come tomorrow."

"Thanks for letting me meet Mother," Cassie said as they walked down the road. "She's lovely."

"She really liked you, didn't she? We should tell her the truth about who you are."

Cassie frowned. "What about her health?"

"I know, but it's not fair of me to keep you from her after all this time, is it?"

"I'm more than happy to keep things as they are, as long as I can keep on seeing her. That means so much to me – you have no idea how much. I'd hate to be the reason something bad happens to her."

"Okay." Tara furrowed her brow. "We won't say anything for now and if you like you can stay with me for a few more nights, but you must promise to leave my stuff alone. And maybe you can come to this party with me, now that I've said I'm going. I don't like telling lies."

Cassie flung her arms around her, something that surprised her again. She was not normally an arm-flinger. "Thank you, Tara. I promise I won't ever enter that room again unless you ask and of course I'll go to the party with you. It would be my honour."

"Sorry for barking at you earlier. I got the job, but they want me to go training in two weeks, so that's the end of that. It's far too soon to sort anything."

"I could help ..."

"Mother's heart is so frail. I couldn't possibly go off and leave a dying woman," Tara continued, ignoring Cassie's comment. "No, I can't go and that's the end of it. I'll turn down the job."

Cassie stood in front of Tara. "Listen to me, I can help! Mary likes me, you said it yourself, and I'm a trained carer, I can do all that stuff in my sleep! I looked after a woman older and frailer than Mary for far longer than a week. I know how to do this; this is my thing!"

Tara bit her lip. "I don't know—"

"How long is the training for?"

"A week. Seven days. From Friday to Friday."

"Go. I'll gladly look after her. I have a whole lifetime to catch up on and you know I have nowhere to be. Do it!"

The hint of a smile danced on Tara's lips. "I would love to see London. You really think it can work?"

"I know it can." Cassie linked Tara and continued down the road. The plan was falling so sweetly into place.

Stopping at the 24/7 to stock up on essentials, the young store assistant glanced up from his phone. "No wine tonight, Mrs?" he asked Tara.

"Not tonight," she said, and Cassie realised she hadn't thought of alcohol all night.

22

TARA

Saturday, 12 November

"Breakfast is ready," Cassie called from the kitchen.

Tara laid her new dress out on her bed. It was nice, but she couldn't wear the same outfit to Barry's birthday party as the interview: he'd already seen her in it. Why did she care what he thought? Her stomach did a little jump.

It's because he sees me.

He'd invited her twice – no, three times – to the party; he surely wanted her there, but she was so bad at judging these things. Cassie would know.

He'd asked her to his party, seemed happy when they met on the train, and he was the one who encouraged her to go for the job. It made her feel warm inside, although she still didn't fancy him.

"I'm sorry for overreacting yesterday," Tara said, taking a seat at the breakfast table, already full of food. "I had a terrible day and I took it out on you."

"That's okay. I was wrong to pour your wine down the sink and go into your room, but it really was my only option at the time, and look, I stayed sober, meaning no hangover, meaning I am ready to face this beautiful Saturday morning. What are your plans for the day?"

"No plans. Usually, I clean up the apartment and wash my clothes, then do the grocery shopping for both me and Mother, but you have all that done. I don't know what I'll do; this has never happened before."

Cassie brought the tea and sat down at the table, her knee bent and foot on the chair. Tara would have loved to be that flexible.

"I was thinking of taking a walk along the coast," Cassie said and took a bite of toast. "It's really stunning along the cliffs, blows away the cobwebs. Would you like to join me?"

Tara helped herself to sausages and bacon. "Maybe, or we could go shopping and you could help me pick something to wear for tonight. I've never been shopping with another woman that wasn't Mother before, and that was a long time ago. The women in the office are always going on about retail therapy and girls' days out, things like that. Personally, I don't understand how constantly buying clothes can be fun, but they seem to enjoy it, so what do you say? Will you come?"

Cassie beamed. "I'd love to."

FOUR HOURS later and laden with branded carrier bags, they stopped for lunch at Milo's Italian restaurant, where the Christmas shopping and party seasons collided, creating a queue that snaked back through the three-storey shopping centre, down the steps and all the way to the exit.

Cassie peered in the window. "Let's go somewhere quieter."

Tara stood her ground. "No. I haven't researched the menu anywhere else. I'm allergic to lots of things."

Cassie squeezed her eyes shut and pinched the bridge of her nose. "Fine. We'll eat here."

"Thank you."

The queue moved ever so slightly.

"So, allergies, huh?" Cassie asked. "What are you allergic to exactly?"

"Dairy, wheat and maybe eggs."

"Jeez, that's a big deal! And, ah – hence the no eggs at breakfast!"

"I'm used to it; it's been like this since I was a child, but I'd be lost without Mother. She bakes using her special ingredients and she cooks dinner every day, with enough over for lunch the day after. Eating out, like this, means researching first, but that rarely happens."

A large party of rosy-faced people in suits and sparkly dresses poured out of the restaurant and they moved up the queue until they were almost inside the door.

"Table for two?" the waiter asked Tara and she nodded.

"Mary cooks for you every day?" Cassie asked. "Like weekends and holidays too?"

"I've never taken a holiday. I, I wouldn't know what to do."

It was a standing joke in the office. Tara Ryan shared her name with an airline yet had never been on an aeroplane. They sneered that she should sell her days off to colleagues who had a life. Those who couldn't get enough time off, which to Tara said a lot about their commitment to the job, yet they were the ones who were popular and promoted.

"I'm sorry," Cassie said. "I shouldn't be asking you these personal questions. It's none of my business."

"No, it's nice to have someone to ... to ask."

"Now, ladies, follow me." The waiter handed them a menu and a wine list each, then showed them to their seats. Tara examined the menu, although she already knew what she wanted. "I'm having the Vegan Classic Pizza, what do you fancy?"

Cassie looked like she might cry.

"Are you okay?" Tara asked.

"Yeah, I need to use the toilet, though. Will you order for me? I'll have the same as you." She dashed to the restroom and the waiter came, tablet in hand.

"Ready to order?"

"My sister is in the bathroom, but I know what she wants."

My sister.

Tara ordered for them both.

"And to drink, madam?"

A crisp white Chardonnay would have been delicious but probably not the best idea with Cassie.

"A jug of iced water, please," Tara said, handing him back the menus and wine lists.

All around the restaurant, people chatted away, not one person dining alone. She wasn't alone either, not today, as

Cassie returned and their orders arrived. Tara tucked in, but Cassie ate so slowly. It was no wonder she was skinny.

"You don't have any allergies?" Tara asked between mouthfuls.

"No, I'm allergic to nothing except litres of vodka." Cassie laughed but it didn't reach her eyes. "I shouldn't joke. No, no food allergies. I'd eat anything and I do. I guess the allergy genes missed me."

Cassie didn't even fill the width of her chair. She looked wrecked in the same hoody, jeans and runners. Nothing Tara owned would fit her, even if she had offered, and all the new clothes in the shopping bags at her feet were for herself. Cassie never asked for anything all morning, except for more cigarettes.

"I should buy you some clothes," she said, expecting Cassie to be overjoyed, but she didn't react.

"No, there's no need, but thank you for the offer," she said.

"You're very slim. I wish I was."

"You are, Tara, you've a great figure but, and I hope you don't mind me saying this, you hide it in clothes that are too old for you and far too big."

Tara's heart dropped. "I like my clothes roomy and comfortable, but the dress I bought today is nice, isn't it?"

Cassie bit her lip. "It was that dress I was talking about, and what you have in those bags. Tara, you're a good-looking woman but you come off like a frump, like you're trying to repel people. You could look a million dollars with a bit of styling and effort."

They both looked over as the waiter brought another bottle of wine to the increasingly animated couple at the table beside them. He showed them the label on the bottle, then poured.

Cassie sighed. "Sorry. I shouldn't have said that about your appearance. Ignore me. I'm on edge because it's tough. It's tough watching people drink wine, knowing I can never touch it again. It seems so ..."

"Unfair?"

"More than that. It seems impossible, like it's never going to get easy. I wonder if it is bigger than me, you know? The drink. Is that my story – will I die alone, drunk on the street?"

That uncomfortable feeling in Tara's stomach from the shower yesterday rose again and what she did next surprised her. She reached out for Cassie's hand. It was cold. "I'm glad you came today. My sister. That won't be your story because you're not alone. You have me."

Cassie squeezed Tara's hand tight and started to sob, proper big sobs that made people stare. "I'm sorry. I never had ... never had any family of my own. It's really nice." She wiped her tears and sat up straight. "Now, enough crying, this is a happy day. There's a party tonight, where did you say it's on?"

"Brooke's – the same bar me and you met. Barry, my boss, it's his birthday and he asked me to come. Barry said—"

Cassie smirked and Tara's face heated before, out of nowhere, the words tumbled out of her mouth. Barry. How he was nice to her in work, how they met on the train – twice, how he offered her a lift. How he organised her promotion. When she finished, Tara realised she was smiling.

"Jeez, Tara. Sounds like he's keen. Do you like him?"

"Yeah, he's kind and funny. I'd like to go to say thanks to

him for being nice to me. A lot of people will be there, and I'm not comfortable in crowds, but I went to the pub the night I met you, so I'm sure I could do it again."

"I mean do you *like him*, like him?"

Did she *like him*, like him? "No, I don't think so anyway. I've never had a boyfriend, so I don't know. What does it feel like to fancy someone?"

Cassie's eyes widened. "Wow, never? Okay. How does it feel? ... Good! It feels good, like you can't think of anything else or anyone else and you can't wait to see them." She stopped. "No, scratch that. That's how it feels to me, but anything I've ever had has been fast and wild and never ended well. What you are describing, I think, that's how it's meant to be."

Tara took a moment to absorb Cassie's words, feeling glad she had asked her sister's opinion on it.

"Look," Cassie said, "I wasn't going to say anything, but will you show me that new dress again?"

Tara passed the largest bag to Cassie, who held up the dress.

"It's not my place to pass judgement," she said, "I know that, but, Holy Mother, it really is a tent."

Tara felt like she had been slapped in the face. Why didn't Cassie say something in the shop? She felt her blood pressure rise.

"It's perfectly fine for me," she said. "I have no interest in dressing like a slut. I am not a piece of meat. Mother says if you put it all out on show that you're asking for it."

"Oh, good Lord." Cassie clapped her hand to her face in despair. "Tara, Mary is an old woman with, ahem, traditional tastes. Do you trust me?"

Tara considered the question, and was surprised by the answer that came out of her mouth. "Yes," she said.

"Right. This is going straight back to the nunnery where it belongs. If the sisters themselves don't cast it off. Let's try again. We'll get you something far more appropriate for a party, for your age, and your fabulous shape, without making you look anything like 'a slut'."

That sounded like a reasonable plan to Tara, and maybe Cassie could get something too. She couldn't figure out what was wrong with offering to buy clothes for her sister earlier, so she said it again. "Then I insist you get a new outfit too."

Cassie lowered her head. "There really is no need. I'm not a charity case."

"I want to. You're my sister."

"Excuse me, madam," the waiter said to Tara. "I am sorry to interrupt, but the manager wishes to talk to you. Urgently."

He guided her through the restaurant, out the back and into a small office, where another man in a shirt and tie sat.

"What is it?" Tara asked.

"Please sit, madam. I'm afraid there has been a serious incident and, by law, we are obliged to inform you before you leave the restaurant."

Cassie. She was in the toilet ages and agitated. She'd robbed someone or something. Tara should have known. How stupid she was for trusting her.

"What did she do?" Tara asked.

The manager scrunched up his nose. "What? Who? No, the incident happened in our kitchen. The pizza served to you was not vegan, nor was it gluten free. Your server just started working here tonight and mixed up your pizzas. Luckily, he realised his mistake and informed us before you left. We wholeheartedly apologise, this has never happened to us before. The meal is obviously complementary and, please, do let us know if there is anything else we can do."

Tara scrambled for words. By right, she should have had a reaction, she should have been violently ill, but she was fine. In fact, she felt great.

23

CASSIE

It was so tempting. As they queued for lunch outside Milo's, the massive window revealed coloured bottles stacked neatly in the restaurant bar and boozy parties in full flow. She wanted to run away with every fibre of her being, but with a night in the pub ahead for Tara's friend Barry tonight, she'd have to be strong. She could do this, make it through the lunch, but when the waiter handed her the wine list, it was too much. In the unisex toilet cubicle, she sat with her head between her knees and focused on her breaths. In for four, out for six. It took everything she had to return a few moments later with a smile on her face. It was excruciating – the bar, the guzzling revellers, the couple at the table beside them who sank two bottles of champagne. It was hell on earth and Cassie despaired if she'd ever be able to handle being sober in this world, but she made it through. She'd stayed sober again.

At 6 p.m., dressed to the nines, they took the short walk to Mary's house. The night was dry and the air felt unseasonably warm. Tara was in great form.

"You look gorgeous," Cassie told her. "How are you feeling since the pizza?"

Tara shrugged. "Really good. I don't understand it. The restaurant must have got the mix-up mixed up."

That seemed unlikely, from the manager's reaction and the waived bill. "What happened the last time you had gluten or dairy?" she asked, as they crossed the main road and headed up the hill.

"I haven't had it since I can remember, so I don't know. We should ask Mother; she'll remember. But it definitely involved a lot of vomiting and toilet visits."

At the garden gate, Cassie took a breath. "Do you think that you don't have those allergies anymore? That you might have outgrown them?"

Tara laughed. "Don't be ridiculous. You can't outgrow allergies. No, the restaurant made a mistake, that's all it was, and we got a free lunch out of it. Now, let's eat again."

"Flowers, ah girls, you shouldn't have," Mary said, accepting the huge pink and lilac bouquet from Cassie, which should have smelled sweet but against the odour in the house was like a mixture of perfume, beef and sewage. She did a double-take. "Well, aren't you pair a sight for sore eyes? You're absolutely stunning. Who are the lucky fellas then?"

Tara giggled like a child. In ways she was totally together – she had a job, a place of her own, a life – albeit limited – but other times, like now, it was like she'd never grown up.

"Mother! There are no fellas. We're going to the work drinks I told you about last night, remember?"

Mary frowned. "Drinks, like alcoholic drinks? You said you were going to a party. You didn't mention that it involved drinks. Are you sure that's a good idea?"

Tara didn't answer.

"I'll be with her, Mrs Ryan," Cassie said to break the silence. "Don't worry. I don't drink."

Mary beamed at Cassie. "Good girl yourself, Joan. Could you have a word with our Tara? She could do with laying off the sauce herself."

"Mother, I told you I have a glass of wine or two now and again. That does not make me have a drink problem."

Mary winked and tipped her nose. "Mother knows what Mother knows. Anyway, enough chatting, the dinner is getting cold on the table. Come on in."

They followed Mary through to the dining room, where the table was set and laden with food and a ginger cat chewed on a piece of meat. Cassie didn't want to think about where the cat might have fetched it from.

"Now girls, you tuck in and I'll have you out of here by eight." Mary put her hand on Tara's, but caught Cassie's eye. "Of course, it means I will be in bed by 8 p.m., which is shocking early for an adult, but Tara is very good to me and nobody deserves a night off more than she."

Cassie dug in. Steak, onions and mushrooms, served with pepper sauce and baked potatoes. It was divine, and she told Mary so. "How was your day, Mrs Ryan?"

The old woman pressed her veiny grey hand against her temple. "Ah, it was fine. I did a little cleaning up, read a bit and watched TV. Same as every other day. Never get old."

"Ah, you're only a young one yet," Cassie said, trying to lighten the mood.

Mary laughed. "Flattery will get you everywhere. Ah, I suppose I'm lucky. Our Tara is a godsend; I honestly don't know what I would do without her." She wiped her eye. "Oh, don't mind me, getting all maudlin. How was your day?"

"We went shopping," Tara said. "It was lovely."

"Lovely." Mary turned her attention back to Cassie. "You were saying you were from Galway, isn't it shocking about that Cherish the Child home?"

Cassie's heart dropped a beat. She was not prepared for this conversation.

"Terrible," she just about managed to answer. "For all involved. I'd imagine it must have been very difficult never seeing your own flesh and blood again."

"It must have been terrible. Different times, though; they did what they had to," Mary said. "Tara, any change of mind on the job?"

The change of subject almost gave Cassie whiplash, but she was relieved to move away from any conversation about the children's home.

"I don't know," Tara said, glancing over at Cassie. "Maybe. There might be a way to figure the job out."

This was good. Very good, but by the look on Mary's face, she didn't agree. "You need to give your head a wobble if you're proceeding with this. After everything that happened with your father?"

Tara stopped eating and put her fork down. "I think Daddy would be happy for me actually, Mother."

"May God forgive you." Mary blessed herself.

"Can I ask what happened to your late husband, Mary?" Cassie asked. "It was a car crash, was it?"

Mary threw Tara a filthy look, then turned her attention to their wedding picture on the wall. "It was, Joan, a car crash. On Christmas Eve and all. Taken by a drunk driver over three times the limit who tried to send me with him. I won't say his name in this house, he is nothing, less than nothing, but he walks the streets today, a free man, while I live this daily purgatory."

"It was the driver not the work that killed him," Tara said under her breath and Mary slammed her fist on the table, making Cassie jump.

"He was working since early that morning. I begged him not to go in on Christmas Eve, but he wouldn't listen. Every day, and remember this was before the times of the internet, every day he was all work, work, work, promotion, promotion, promotion. He was never happy, always wanted more. It's where Tara got it – he was all or nothing and so bloody tunnel-visioned. That Christmas Eve I begged him to stay home, but he wouldn't listen, so I jumped in the car and went with him. The only mercy is that Tara here wasn't with us when that man crashed into us out of nowhere."

"I'm sorry," Cassie said.

Mary nodded. "It is what it is, but I think my darling Frank RIP would mind his only daughter going down the same road that he did. I think he would mind a lot."

Tara excused herself to go to the toilet and Mary's eyes filled with tears. "Joan, you will look after her, won't you? And don't let her drink too much. She likes to think she's Miss Independent but she's shocking innocent and I fear that someone will take advantage." She lowered her voice. "To be honest, I always thought she was a bit slow. She'd believe black was white."

Cassie tapped Mary's hand. "I'll look out for her, don't worry. Now, can I make the tea? I would like to say thanks to you for inviting me into your home."

Mary's face relaxed. "That would be lovely, and you won't tell Tara I said she's slow, will you? I don't want her to be upset with me."

Cassie closed an imaginary zip over her mouth. "Mum's the word, I totally understand. My own mother ..." She dropped her head. "My own mother is long gone, so it's so nice to spend time with you."

Mary lit up. "Well, in that case, come tomorrow for Sunday lunch. That's if you have no other plans."

"I don't have plans and, honestly, I love being here. But I really don't want to overstay my welcome or step on any toes, and if Tara doesn't want me to come ..."

They both looked to Tara, who had come back to the room. "What?"

"Joan is coming for Sunday lunch tomorrow," Mary said. "Now, you girls better get off, enjoy life while you can. Put on the telly there, Joan, and make yourself comfortable while Tara helps me with my nightly duties."

Cassie cleared the dishes, taking them to the adapted sink in the kitchen. The white cat rubbed against her leg, but she kicked him away. Dirty creatures. With dinner cleared and all the dishes cleaned up, she viewed the photo gallery on the wall. Photo after photo of Mary, Frank and Tara. At the beach, outside a church, smiling into a frame. Mary was a good-looking woman, tall and slim with hair as short as her skirt. Frank was dashing, too, and together they made a handsome couple.

"Almost ready," Tara called from the bedroom. "Giving Mother a little massage before we go. There's plenty of time."

"Take your time." Cassie moved on to the next photo, which was a full-length one of Mary sitting on the bonnet of a car. The style of her – she was stunning, like something from a magazine in her tank top and mini skirt. Her shoes were brown and high and ... Cassie almost collapsed. Brown, laced and wooden heels. She looked back at the car. That distinctive shape of it.

It was a red Mini.

"That's Mother settled for the night," Tara said when she returned to the room. Then, catching sight of Cassie, "You look like you saw a ghost. What happened?"

"Nothing, just tired. Long day."

Cassie couldn't think. She'd had it all wrong, thinking They had taken Tara and sold her off. It was Mary who took Tara that day from the house. Mary who abducted Tara for herself. It was Mary.

Your problem is you dive in. Take a breather and use your head. Decide, don't react.

THE JOURNEY into the city centre was a quiet one, the only sound the taxi radio and the driver lining up his next fare after them. Cassie's head was exploding with this discovery, but she would have to pull herself together for tonight. The photo changed everything, and yet it changed nothing. The end goal was still the same – to make the house hers – and the way to get there unchanged: being useful, staying sober and keeping her mouth shut.

"You are very quiet, Cassie. Are you okay?"

Cassie nodded, searching for words.

"I know what's wrong with you," Tara whispered, as the car pulled up on Kildare Street and they got out. "I know what happened back in Mother's when I left the room and I know why you don't want to talk about it."

Cassie's stomach dropped. Had Tara been watching her? "What do you mean?"

Tara turned to her. "When I was gone to the toilet, I heard what Mother said to you about the alcohol and me being innocent. You think less of me now, don't you? You think I'm slow."

"No, I think you are anything but," Cassie said. "The last few days have been a lot, you know?"

Tara squeezed her arm. "I do, and thank you. I'm so glad you came with me tonight."

Cassie pulled her new moss-green coat around her shoulders – it was one of those ones quilted like a duvet with a hood and belt – and kept her head down as she approached the door of Brooke's. A bouncer with a scar on his cheek stood at the entrance, chewing gum and scanning the street. She prayed it wasn't the same one as the last night she was here, though she couldn't remember what he looked like. She looked different herself of course, but she linked Tara's arm just in case he recognised her. As they approached the door, he took a step towards them, stopping Cassie's heart as he looked them up and down.

"Welcome, ladies," he said in a strong Dublin accent, then opened the door for them to enter.

Inside, the place was stifling hot and packed tight with sparkly women wearing too much makeup and fake tan and open-shirted men. By the looks of them they'd been here a while. Christmas music played too loud and a group of people in Christmas jumpers and head boppers did shots at the bar. Oh, what Cassie would have given to join them.

One won't hurt.

"I'll get us a drink," Tara shouted in Cassie's ear. "What do you want?"

A fucking litre of vodka, Cassie thought.

"A Coke please," she said.

Tara gave Cassie her coat to hold and joined the queue for the bar. She looked incredible. They'd returned the frumpy-nun clothes and she picked a black sparkly jumpsuit that emphasised her figure instead. Cassie got an outfit too, along with a curly blow-dry in this high-class hairdresser and a makeover, although that was a freebie off a pensioner in some dive of a pharmacy. She argued she didn't need half of it and for Tara to stop spending her money, but Tara insisted, saying she wanted to because she had no friends to do all this with before and nothing else to spend her money on.

Cassie hated charity. It seemed she was supposed to suck it up and accept it, considering her whole life was made of handouts, but she hated it. For once, she would love to have something to call her own.

She pulled at the hem of her emerald green bodycon dress that Tara – in her usual blunt way – said she had the figure for, but was a bit too old to wear. Still, she paid for it along with the silver sandals, silver hoop earrings and chain she was wearing now. She finished the look with a black pleather jacket.

To her left a circle of women clinked champagne flutes and whooped. The bubbles danced in front of her and everything started to spin. This was too much too soon. She inhaled deeply and counted to five.

Higher power, higher power.

Her heart rate slowed and she came back to the present much quicker this time. It wasn't that ridiculous to think that when Mary passed away she would leave her house to Tara, and Tara would give it to Cassie, being her one and only sibling. People had a tendency to crawl out of the woodwork at the sniff of an inheritance, but there would only be two standing to benefit in this case.

What would she do with the house when it became hers? Very little. It already felt like a home with its old-style décor and floral patterns, but those cats had to go. They gave her PTSD after everything that had happened. She'd move straight in and take walks on the strand. Would she get a dog? Oh, how she would love a big old mongrel, but looking after herself was probably more than enough responsibility for now. She might even take over cooking duties for Tara or, she thought with a flutter, she could get a job. With an address, and being clean, she could find work, although she wouldn't go back into caring. Something physical, though. She needed to be busy. For once, she would have something of her own and prospects for the future.

A woman holding a champagne flute fell against her shoulder, breaking her trance.

"Watch where you're going," Cassie snapped.

"Sorry," the woman slurred and steadied herself. It was the tall one with the black Lego hair from Tara's office, the stupid bitch who had told her to get back to work, wearing a tiny sparkly white dress that made her look like a deranged Barbie doll. She staggered on ridiculous heels back to the circle of cackling women.

Tara was still waiting to be served at the bar. A bald stocky man, wearing blue jeans and black T-shirt, tipped her on the shoulder. She turned around, smiled and chatted to him. He called the barman, who took their order. With two drinks, Tara fought her way back through the crowds to Cassie, the man following behind with a pint of stout. She handed Cassie her drink and sipped her own through a straw from a fishbowl. The man smiled and nodded at

Cassie, then took a mouthful of his black pint, the cream settling on his upper lip. Cassie waited for introductions, but Tara said nothing.

"Gin and tonic. Good choice," Cassie said to break the silence. "And you can't go wrong with a pint of Guinness."

"Please don't tell Mother. She'll think I'm an alcoholic on the streets. No offence."

Cassie laughed. She should have been annoyed but she couldn't help it. Tara was as subtle as a sledgehammer. "None taken. Aren't you going to introduce us?"

"Sorry." Tara blushed. "This is my manager. Barry."

"Guilty as charged." Barry's eyes twinkled and he offered his hand. "Pleasure to meet you, and you are?"

He had a fine solid handshake and there was something nice about him, like a counsellor. Something very warm.

"Who am I? Great question." She nudged Tara for back-up, but she stood in silence, examining her shoes. Barry raised an eyebrow, waiting on an answer.

Who was she tonight? A friend, a work colleague, a sister? Nah, not a sister but Tara needed to speak up and tell her quickly. Barry took a sip from his pint and glanced around the bar.

"I'm Tara's friend, Cassie," she said when it was clear Tara wasn't going to help out. It would have to do. "Are you having a nice birthday?"

"Yeah, it's great so far," he said. "There's a good crowd and the cake was gorgeous."

The way he looked at Tara made Cassie smile. He was infatuated. "Sorry, there's none left. I would have kept you a slice if I'd known you were coming."

These strange lovebirds need space, she thought, so she excused herself to go to the bathroom.

"Will you get the drinks in on the way back?" Tara pulled a €50 note from her bag and handed it to her. Cassie agreed, taking the money, but she couldn't get to the toilets quick enough.

It was like being in a brothel. Green velvet interior, black tiles and ornate full-length mirror with condom machines and Pleasure Zone items on sale. She barely recognised her reflection. She looked well, but Tara had a point about her dress. It was very short. A line of satin-padded cubicle doors swung empty and she chose the last one beside the mirror. The door was barely closed when the sound of the busy pub flooded in.

"Did you see her?" one woman said in a Dublin 4 affected accent. "It's pathetic."

"I think she looks really well," answered another in a softer voice.

"She looks like the fool that she is. Imagine showing up at a party you're not invited to. No doubt the freakshow will shrink back into her shell like she always does. It's not right to be like that. Weirdo."

"Leave her alone, Tara's okay."

Cassie's ears pricked up. The women clip-clopped into cubicles and doors slammed shut.

"Here, Joan, throw me over some loo paper."

Joan. Was this the Joan, her alter ego? The one who spilled Tara's coffee and broke her cup?

"Catch." A toilet roll flew through the air, a white paper kite behind it, and for a minute Cassie thought it was coming for her, but it hit the wall of the cubicle to her right and landed on the ground.

"Cheers, Lucy. I'm sorry, but it's not right, the way Baldy Barry is pretending to be interested her so he can get laid. I hear they're taking odds."

"Where did you hear that rubbish?"

"It's only because he wants a bit of what's going. I'm telling you, he's no interest in her and she's not right in the head. She says nothing to no one for years, then acts like she's all that at the summer party. I heard Leo won five grand for riding her. I wonder how much Baldy will get?"

"I felt sorry for her, to be honest, when I found out what happened. She was so drunk."

"She knew exactly what she was doing; she pretends to be a retard but she's a conniving bitch. Bet Barry is filling her with drink as we speak."

There was silence.

"Don't say that disgusting 'r' word ever again," the woman called Lucy said, after what seemed like forever. "My brother has special needs and I hate that word. You know what? I think you're jealous because you've had a thing for Leo for years. The whole office knows you do, so don't take it out on her, okay? You're sick because you were sleeping with Leo at the time and he did the dirty with her and you can't figure out what she has that you don't. It must be killing you."

"What? No, I wasn't."

A toilet flushed and a cubicle door opened. "You've been sleeping with Leo Harris for ages and everyone knows it. If anyone is a conniving bitch, it's you."

"Jeez, Lucy, chill," Joan said. "I'm sorry, okay? Let's not ruin our night. Here, let's order another bottle of champagne. Sod it, the company is paying for it."

"No, thanks. I don't drink with lowlife and I'm suddenly no longer thirsty."

The main door opened and closed.

"Fuck off, then." It was Joan, talking to herself. Cassie waited for her to leave her cubicle, then opened her door. Yes, there was the Lego-haired cow from earlier, the one that told Tara to get back inside the building. Cassie smiled at her and turned on the tap, keeping her eyes firmly on the mirror. "Joan, is it?"

"Uhm, yes. And you are?"

Cassie grabbed the woman by the throat so fast she gasped, then slammed her up against the tiled wall with a thump. "None of your business. Who were you talking about with your friend just then?"

She flailed and Cassie pushed her harder. "Who were you talking about?"

"Tara," she croaked.

"Tara who?" Cassie pushed harder and she whimpered.

"Ryan. Tara Ryan."

Cassie let go of her and she staggered, holding her throat and gasping for air.

"What were you saying about her?"

"Nothing, psycho."

Cassie drove her fist into the woman's stomach so hard she knocked against the tiled wall and fell onto the ground. "You have picked the wrong day to mess with me. I said what happened to her?"

The woman cowered as Cassie stood over her, fist raised and her blood boiling. The outer door to all of the bathrooms swung open, letting the Christmas music in, and Cassie put her finger over her mouth. "This never happened, and you stay away from my sister or I will break your legs. Understand?"

Joan nodded. Cassie passed another woman rushing in

in stilettos. "Oh my God, Joan. Are you okay? What happened?"

"Your friend had a little too much of something," Cassie said, tapping her nose. "She'll be okay, but you might want to keep an eye on her."

24

TARA

Barry was acting weird, staring at the floor and glancing up at Tara when he thought she wasn't looking. Her drink was long gone and she wished Cassie would hurry back from the toilets and get her a fresh gin and tonic. The first one went down very nicely.

He talked to her on the train when she didn't want him to, but now, when she needed him to, he hadn't said a word. So many of their colleagues were here for his birthday, scattered at tables and standing around. He should have been mingling, but he stayed with her in silence, like the cat got his tongue.

"Are you having a good night?" she asked.

"Yes, I am. And, Tara." He blushed. "You look seriously stunning. I hope it's okay to say that."

"Thank you. Yeah, it is okay. You look very smart yourself," she said.

Barry did a funny move that made Tara laugh, then polished off his pint and held up his glass. "Another one? G&T, isn't it?"

She examined the glass with just a slice of lemon left in it. "No, thanks. Cassie is getting one for me."

"I don't know if your friend is coming back anytime soon," he said, "and I'm going to the bar anyway. Let me get you a drink."

"No thanks, honestly, but thank you."

His shoulders slumped. "If you're sure, so. I'll wait until she comes back. Did you say she's a friend?"

Tara nodded. "Yes, a friend."

"She must be a good one because you gave her €50 note without blinking. I wish I had friends like that."

At that moment, the door of the toilets flew open and Cassie came charging out, grabbing Tara by the arm.

"Hey," Barry said. "What are you doing?"

Cassie was red and panting. "We're leaving. Come on, Tara."

Barry stood between them. "Whoa, calm down. What happened?"

Cassie glanced at Tara, then back to Barry, then back again. "I can't explain it now, Tara, but please trust me, we need to leave!"

"Why?" Tara asked, the speed of the conversation making her dizzy.

Cassie whispered in her ear. "Food poisoning, it's brutal. I need to get home. I need to get out of here."

Barry turned his back to Cassie and faced Tara. "Tara, what do you want to do? I would like you stay for my party, but it's your decision."

Tara bit her lip. She wanted to stay, but Cassie was dancing, holding her stomach. If food poisoning was anything like her allergies, it was horrendous. Mother told her stories she didn't want to recall.

She put her glass on the table beside them. "Sorry, Barry, I have to go. Have a good night and Happy Birthday." She kissed his cheek and he turned puce.

Cassie took her by the hand, and they pushed through the crowd, out the door and past the bouncer, who wished them a safe journey home. Back at the apartment, after a tumultuous taxi ride home, Cassie had a cigarette on the balcony, which must have helped settle her stomach because a few minutes later she was sitting drinking coffee on the couch with Tara, both of them in their new matching Christmas pyjamas they'd bought on a mad impulse while shopping earlier.

"How are you feeling now?" Tara asked.

"Better, thanks. Sorry for ruining your night."

"You didn't. I was having a nice time, but I don't fit in with those people. Apart from Barry, nobody even said hello to me. What did you think of Barry?"

Cassie clenched her teeth into a smile. "He seems nice but ... can I be honest?"

"Please do. That's why I asked."

"I don't like him; something seems very off."

"Like what?"

"I don't know, but something. I don't think he'd be good for you."

Tara was surprised at how disappointed she felt at Cassie's reaction. "He's been nice to me since ... Doesn't matter, it's all in the past."

Cassie pulled her legs up under her with ease. "Since what?"

She didn't want to talk about it, but Cassie moved closer. "You know you can tell me anything, right? Did something happen at work?"

Cassie voice was so steady, her eyes so understanding, that Tara started to talk.

"It was the summer party." Tara took a deep breath. "I didn't want to be at there," she said, the words spilling out for the very first time. "It was pointless pretending to like people and wanting to spend time with them outside work when they ignored me every day inside work. These social events happen two or three times a year, and the office would be alive with gossip after – who slept with who, who fell asleep in their dinner – but I had no interest in that stuff. I got on with my job, Monday to Friday, and nobody bothered me. Until last summer, it wasn't a problem, but they made this one mandatory. I had no choice. It was the Partners Plus Beach Party Bonanza in the Heights Hotel, very fancy. A band played holiday tunes, there was fake sand, deckchairs and a free bar. I thought if I showed up someone would talk to me, but nobody did. It was awkward standing at the bar on my own, so I had a few drinks to help me relax, then a few more. I don't normally dance but I must have been drunk because there I was, dancing, and then I knocked against a table and spilled all the drinks on it. They were so irate, but it was a free bar, so I just went and got them more at the bar. Looking back, that was the right time to call a taxi and go home, I know that now, but I wasn't thinking straight. It felt like I was in someone else's shoes wearing someone else's face." She paused and looked down at her hands. "I don't remember much of the evening after that."

"You blacked out?" Cassie asked.

"No, not blacked out. It wasn't all dark, there are bits. Flashes. One second, I'm doing shots at the bar, the next I'm crying in the toilets and someone is minding me. My last memory is being led up a wide golden staircase, like one from a fairy-tale.

"'No, I don't want to ... I need to go home ... Mother will be worried ...' I thought I said but must have imagined it because I woke up the next morning in a hotel room," she lowered her voice, "naked with Mr Harris's Russian hands and Roman fingers all over me."

Cassie gasped. "Oh, hun."

"I know," Tara said. "I was a slut. My head hurt so bad, and I asked him to stop, but he told me that because he was a married man, and I had seduced him, doing it again made sense. I owed him, he said. He said if he got caught by his wife, he was in trouble anyway. It was me who had made him commit adultery."

"What did you do?" Cassie asked. "I hope you didn't listen."

"I let him have sex with me, of course I did. I didn't want to but what he said made sense – I'd made him commit adultery and if his wife found out, he was in trouble either way. It made complete sense. He was nice, in a way, kept telling me how beautiful I was, but it hurt so much that I picked a spot on the ceiling and counted until he rolled off me. After that he got dressed and left, asking me not to tell anyone – not that I would. I didn't want anyone to know what I had done."

"I'm so sorry... did he use protection? Condoms?"

"Oh yes, there was one on the floor and then the one he used, so he used two anyway. I put them in the bin, then left as fast as I could. Once I got back home, I scrubbed myself for ages in the shower. I felt so dirty, I had slept with another woman's husband."

Cassie's eyes filled with tears. "Tara, it wasn't your fault, it was his! You were drunk and he took advantage."

"No," Tara said firmly. "It was my fault. I drank too much and I jeopardised his marriage and our jobs."

It was her fault and her responsibility. Word had spread fast in the office. Tara never confirmed it – loose lips sink ships, Mother always said. Joan hadn't bothered with her before that, but afterwards she turned really nasty. They all did. It must have been strange for them to think that a senior partner like Mr Harris would be interested in someone like her, though she wished he'd never set eyes on her. HR had called her in and asked if she was okay, which she found strange, too. Someone had made an anonymous complaint, they said. And they just wanted to remind her that relationships between management and employees were against company policy and considered highly unethical. Tara knew what that meant – they could both be sacked and Leo Harris's marriage would be over – so she hadn't said anything. What if it had become a scandal and made the news? Mother would have been so disappointed. Besides, she didn't want to think about any of it. He'd say hello when he passed in work but other than that life went on. Tara decided it was the last work party she'd ever go to. And then she got on with her life.

Cassie placed her mug on the floor and took Tara's hand in hers, rubbing it gently. "Oh, love. I am so sorry that happened to you."

Tara felt a huge weight lift, one she didn't know was there until now. Her sister knew her biggest secret. "You must think I'm terrible, a real slut."

"Come here," Cassie said and pulled her into a tight hug. "There's no call for that hateful word, not ever. I'm never going to let anyone hurt you ever again. I promise."

25

CASSIE

Wednesday, 23 November

They said it took twenty-eight days to create a new habit but, after only fourteen days, Cassie was well into her new routine, and loving it. With the breakfast dishes put away and the floors washed, she set out for her morning walk along the beach, letting the calm waves kiss the new walking boots that Tara insisted on buying for her. The day was clear and crisp, and the spray of the seawater made her feel alive. With three weeks to Christmas, the shops along the promenade glistened with their bright lights and she searched for the year's music highlights on her phone. What a year that was. Sober, drunk, sober again, and of course meeting her sister. Year? That was all in the last month!

Tara had agreed to let her sleep on the couch until she found a job and this week she'd applied for two positions, not in care work, even though that's what she loved, but housekeeping in the two local hotels. Judging by the warm reception she got when she dropped her CV in, she was even hopeful she'd get a call, although her priority now lay with visiting Mary while Tara was away.

Mary. The only fly in this ointment. She had deteriorated in the last few weeks, getting more tired by the day, especially since Tara told her that she was taking the job and going to the training in London. That did not go down well at all. Mary argued, but Tara held her ground against one colossal guilt trip, and Cassie was proud of her.

"You can't leave me here alone. Who will look after me?" Mary cried.

"Joan is going to call on you every day, Mother. You won't be alone."

"You're a selfish madam, always were," Mary spat out.

Cassie found it tough to hold her tongue, but she was getting used to it. So many times, the truth almost burst out over dinner or when she was alone with Tara, but each time she swallowed her words.

At Portmarnock she left the strand and climbed onto the cliffs. The view was breath-taking and an aeroplane left a white fluffy trail in the sky. Two days until Tara took flight for the first time, and she couldn't have been happier for her. Her first time abroad, her first time on a plane. Cassie thought this strange until she realised that she had never been abroad either. How lovely it would be to be heading off to somewhere hot across the sea, but she couldn't complain. She had a roof over her head and, right now, this incredible view.

The sky turned grey over the dunes ahead, and the waves swelled, a sign that heavy rain was on the way. She'd become good at judging the weather from her daily walks, better than the weather forecast on the TV, which gave cloud but no rain this morning. If she turned back now, she might make it home before the deluge. She checked the time on her phone – 12:07. It was going to be a very long afternoon unless ... She fingered the set of keys for Mary's house that Tara had got cut and given to her this morning, along with keys to her own apartment and a fifty-euro note. Cassie didn't want to take it, but Tara insisted. For emergencies while she was away, she said, and maybe to buy something nice for Mary and herself too. Mmm, something nice.

She crossed the road and the familiar smell of hops heralded the pub that almost toppled her when she first arrived. She stopped outside and felt the money in her pocket. Next door, a pink-haired young woman in an apron came out, her arms full with ivy wreaths, and greeted Cassie. "It's beginning to look a lot like Christmas," she said and arranged the wreaths along the front of the flower shop. Cassie had never noticed the shop before.

"It sure is." Cassie walked on before turning back. There were two homes that looked nothing like Christmas – Tara's and Mary's. They said Frank loved Christmas, and it was too painful for them to put up decorations, but maybe a reminder of him would cool the atmosphere between them. She chose a vibrant, full green wreath with gold baubles and blood red holly berries for €30. An investment, a splurge, too expensive to buy two.

"Isn't it beautiful?" the florist said, handing her back €20 change.

The sky was almost black and the rain was spitting by the time Cassie let herself in to Mary's house, the wreath concealed behind her back. She wasn't due until dinner tonight, but Mary didn't go anywhere.

The smell hit her immediately. Would she ever get used to it? The white cat observed her from the landing, halfway up the stairs, but didn't budge. About to take off her coat, muted voices came from the living room. Was that ... a man? She froze to the spot.

"That's the script for the painkillers, Mrs Ryan. Is there anything else I can help you with before I leave?" said a velvet-smooth voice. Definitely a man.

"Nothing, Doctor, and I keep telling you, call me Mary."

The doctor. Cassie should have called before calling in unannounced; she didn't expect Mary to have company.

"And you're sure you're comfortable?" he asked. "I can increase your dosage, even though you are out of the woods."

"Thank you, Doctor but I'm managing, thanks to my Tara. She's an angel, Doctor. I don't know where I'd be without her."

Oh no, no, no. Cassie felt a sneeze come on but caught it in time to make it barely a grunt.

"What was that?" the man asked and Cassie held her breath.

"I said she's an angel, Doctor. My Tara," Mary answered, louder this time.

"Oh, she is. Well, Mrs Ryan – Mary – you're doing so well I don't think I need to see you for a month. You're amazing, Mary; you'll outlive us all."

Cassie crept to the living-room door which was ajar and peeped through the gap between it and the frame. Mary was right in front of her, looking like a different person. Sitting upright and smiling, with a full set of teeth, and was that lipstick on her?

Mary glanced towards the door and Cassie jumped back into the hall. She needed to get out of there. Tiptoeing to the front door, she exited, easing the door closed behind her. Up the street, her heart banging in her chest, her phone beeped, making her jump. A message from Tara.

> Hope your day is going well. I got my plane tickets. It's all happening now.

Cassie turned and watched as a man came out of Mary's house; fully suited and carrying a medical bag. He waved back to the house, then clicked his key and got into a sparkling Mercedes parked outside the house that she had been too preoccupied with her wreath to notice on her way in. Cassie watched him drive past her before she turned away from the house and headed for the apartment. Another message.

> All thanks to you, sister.

So, Mary was doing well. Not the news she'd hoped for, but Tara would be delighted. It would let her go off on her trip with no worries.

Cassie started to text.

Great news about Mary, then deleted the text. Let Mary tell her the news herself. Instead, she replied:

> You deserve it. xx

"TELL her that the vegetables have real dairy butter on them." Mary had been in a foul humour since Cassie gave her the wreath. Tara warned it wouldn't be received well and she was right. Mary had forced a thank you but left it on the floor by the front door.

"Mother, why would you do that? You know I can't have real butter. Is it because I'm going away? It's only for seven nights and Joan is going to look after you. Anyway, whether you like it or not, I'm going."

Cassie couldn't find words since she'd arrived for dinner tonight and found the old woman back to looking exhausted and sounding feeble. No sign of lipstick or teeth.

"The doctor was here, Joan," she said to Cassie. "He said I took a turn for the worse, never saw anyone go downhill as quick. Asked if my daughter would move in to look after me, seeing as I am so near the end. I didn't tell him she was leaving the country for a week; I was too ashamed to say she'd leave me to die alone. That's what I fear most, Joan. Dying alone."

Tara wiped her mouth and threw her napkin on the table.

Cassie had enough. "In that case I won't visit – I'll stay with you altogether. I am due holidays from work," she lied, "and I'll take them next week. I'll move in while Tara is gone and look after you."

Mary's mouth hung open. "I couldn't possibly ask—"

"No, it's settled. Tara will go on the trip that is already organised and paid for, and I can take care of you here."

The old woman eyeballed her, but Cassie held her gaze. "Alright? Tara will get the break she so badly needs and see a little bit of the world. You want her to be happy, as her mother, don't you?"

Mary frowned. "But what if I die?"

"Nonsense, you'll be grand, sure won't you have me 24/7? I helped look after my own gran; you'll be in good hands and Tara will be just across the pond. I'll tell you what – why don't we have a dry run tomorrow night, me and you, and if everything goes well, Tara can head off on Friday without anybody having to worry."

Mary didn't answer.

"Great, so," Cassie said. "That's sorted."

26

TARA

Thursday, 24 November

Being in the office late was a new experience. At 5:45 p.m., Christmas music played in the next cubicle followed by a flurry of activity in the walkway.

John left at 5:30 p.m. but arrived back to his desk in a red and white Christmas jumper and fake antlers. The colour drained from his face when he saw Tara.

"What's going on?" she asked.

"Eh ... ah, impromptu drinks. Not organised at all, you know. Spur of the moment."

A cackling hen threw her head around the cubicle wall. "Brooke's or Steers, John – where do you want to go? I put it in the WhatsApp – oh, hi Tara. What are you still doing in the office?"

"Preparing for my trip to London tomorrow," she said,

and the woman skulked away. Tara swallowed hard and checked the details of her flight again. There was no point in getting upset over being left out of work dos or WhatsApp groups or whatever it was they were doing because she didn't want to be with them anyway, and she had more exciting things to look forward to. Tomorrow night she would be in the air on her first flight ever. Her stomach was doing somersaults; leaving Mother was a risk, but the overwhelming emotion was excitement. Her colleagues could party all they wanted; she was going on an adventure.

She sent her documents to the printer. Flying out from Dublin Airport at 9:10 p.m., the plan was to come to work tomorrow morning as always, then maybe share a six-seater to the airport with Barry and the new employees who were going with them, and whom she had yet to meet. A new opportunity to make friends before this place contaminated them – she was going to take it.

"Hey, what has you here at this time?" It was Barry in a mistletoe tie. He was in on the secret party too, which hurt more than she wanted to admit.

"Sorting the last few details for tomorrow. Are you heading out somewhere?"

"Um, yeah. A few of us are going for drinks. You got your passport, I heard."

Tara held up the small wine book. "Sorted."

Getting the passport had been weird. There was an issue with her birth cert but Kerrie in accounts had a brother who was high up in the passport office and a call was made. "It's not what you know," she said when she delivered the passport by hand to Tara's desk, "it's who you know."

Barry sighed. "Listen, I'm not in the mood for a mad one

like this crew. I don't suppose you fancy a quiet one some-where else?" He adjusted his tie, a little awkwardly. "As friends?"

Tara did fancy one, she very much fancied one. The deal was she was to stay away from her mother for the evening to give Cassie a trial run on her own ahead of the trip. The problem was that left her with nothing to do and no one to do it with. She thought she'd stay back and organise the trip but that took all of ten minutes and the printouts weren't even needed.

"I'd like that," she said.

Joan poked her head into the shared cubicle. "Are you coming, Barry?"

"No, you guys go on without me. I've a few things to do here first."

Joan looked from Tara to Barry and back again, then tutted and left.

<hr />

"Cheers," Barry said, accepting the pint in the quiet pub, his tie loosened. A few old men sat at the otherwise empty bar. "How are you feeling about the training?"

Tara took a sip of her third G&T. They were going down nicely. "I'm looking forward to it but I'm nervous too. I've never been on a plane before."

Barry sat back in the booth, his arm almost around her. "First timer? Wow. Don't worry, there's nothing to be nervous about. Flying, I mean. It's safer than driving, and I'll be with you all the way."

"No, I'm not nervous about flying, I've already decided I'll like that."

He smiled.

"No, it's because I look after my mother. She's very ill and I visit her every night after work. There's only me, so if I don't do it nobody does – not that I mind." Tara couldn't believe the words were coming so freely, but she liked speaking like this and, what's more, Barry was listening to her.

"Sorry to hear your mum isn't well. It's a worry when they get older, isn't it?" He cleared his throat and stroked his tie. "My mother passed away last year after a long battle with Alzheimer's. It was very tough."

He took a large gulp from his pint.

"I'm sorry for you, Barry. You've only one mother, right?"

"Yeah." He cleared his throat. "Only one mother. Is there someone to look after yours while you're gone?"

"Yeah, Cassie's going to take care of her."

"Is that the woman who was at my birthday bash?"

"Yes, that's her. She's very good with Mother."

Barry went quiet and Tara felt the atmosphere change. She scrambled for what wrong thing she'd said; there was surely something.

"Tara, can I ask you a question? This Cassie, who is she?"

Maybe it was the gin or the company or having someone actually ask, but before she quite knew what she was doing, Tara spilled it all. The DNA, the first meeting, the alcoholism, the homelessness, everything. Barry never took his eyes off her.

"So, that's who she is," Tara said, taking a long drink of the last of her G&T. "She is my sister."

Barry reached for her hand and she let him take it, which should have been weird but wasn't. It was lovely. "Tara, I know it's not my place to tell you what to do, but are you sure this is a good idea? You know this woman a few weeks and she's already living in your apartment, wearing your clothes, spending your money, and now she's going to take care of your mother while you are out of the country. Does that not strike you as strange?" He shook his head. "I'm sorry to say this, but it sounds like she's taking advantage of you."

Tara pulled her hand away, the familiar feeling of being underestimated returning and snapping her from her buzz. "She is not taking advantage of me, thank you very much. She's my sister who's had a hard life and she is trying to do better. She has nowhere else to go and I'm able to help her, so I should. Plus, she's helping me by taking care of Mother, who likes her – and she is an excellent judge of character."

Barry shook his head. "Oh Tara. Oh no, no, no, no. This stinks. How do you know it's even her DNA she used and someone didn't spit into a cup for her? Did you even google her?"

Tara glowered at him. Barry was getting on her nerves now and she didn't like where this conversation was going. "Of course, I googled her and found nothing. There was nothing online about her, nothing on social media or anything."

"Nothing at all. Isn't that strange?"

"Hardly, Barry. She's homeless! She'd hardly be thinking about Instagram moments when she was on the streets, plus, if you google me, you'll find nothing either. Not everyone lives their lives online."

"Fair point. Did she show you any identification?"

He was really annoying now. "No, but I'll ask if it means we can change the subject. I thought we were out for a sociable drink. I was enjoying my time with you until you started with the third degree and now I need another drink."

Barry rubbed his head. "Okay, but there is one last thing. I wasn't going to say anything, but I think it's better you know. The night of my birthday party, before Cassie had that sudden bout of food poisoning, Joan said she was attacked in the toilets, completely unprovoked, by this crazy woman who tried to choke her. She didn't want to press charges, but she could have. Who do you think that was?"

Tara didn't want to hear any more. "On second thoughts, forget the drink. I want to go home."

"I didn't mean to upset you," Barry said. "I'll go with you. I'll order us a cab."

"I can get myself home, I'm not a child," she said, but Barry insisted.

"I asked you out and I'll make sure you get home safe."

The taxi stopped outside Tara's apartment and Barry paid the driver. "I'll come upstairs with you and call a cab from there, if that's okay. I need to use the toilet."

Tara reluctantly agreed and was rooting for her keys in her bag when Cassie opened the apartment door. "Tara ... Barry?"

Barry followed Tara inside. "Hi Cassie. Making sure this one got home safe; she's had a little too much to drink. Can I use your loo?"

Too much to drink? Tara felt completely sober.

"Of course. Down the hall, first door on the right," Cassie answered. "Coffee?"

"Please." Barry left the room.

Cassie sauntered to the kitchen and switched on the kettle. Tara followed her.

"I can't believe what you did," she whispered across the counter.

Cassie looked confused but unphased. She retrieved

three mugs from the cupboard over her head and put a spoon of instant coffee into each. "What? What did I do?"

"I know everything," Tara said. "Don't take me for a fool and just tell me."

"Aha, you mean the cat going missing." Cassie shrugged. "He's a cat. That's what cats do. I told Mary not to tell you and worry you. Sure, he's probably back and all by now."

"What are you on about?" Tara asked. Now it was her turn to feel confused. "I mean you attacking Joan at the party. Why, what happened to the cat?"

"The black one got out, but he'll be back. They always come back."

Sooty.

"What did Barry say about me?" Cassie asked. The kettle clicked itself off and she poured the boiling water into the mugs, stirring them individually.

"He claims someone attacked Joan in the toilets the night of his birthday. Was it you?"

Cassie stopped stirring and her eyes narrowed. "Oh my God, the little weasel. I don't trust him one bit. Please tell me nothing happened between you two."

"Nothing happened."

"Good, because there's something you need to know."

"All okay, girls?" It was Barry back in the room. "Where's that coffee?"

All three sat together in the living area, sipping their drinks and making small talk. "I hope your stomach settled, Cassie," Barry said, "after that terrible bout of food poisoning you got at my party. Where was it you said you were from again?"

"I didn't."

"Mayo. She's from Mayo," Tara answered, sipping the coffee and feeling more sober by the minute.

"Ah Mayo," Barry said. "Where exactly? I have cousins down there; you might know them? The O'Briens?"

Cassie played with her mug. "Hardly. I was raised in a children's home."

After the coffee and alcohol, Tara's bladder was fit to burst, so she made her apologies and went to the toilet. She barely had her trousers pulled back up when raised voices came from the kitchen and she rushed up to find Barry cornered by Cassie.

"What's going on?" she demanded, and Cassie jumped back.

"He's accusing me of all sorts, the little asshole!" she said.

Barry straightened himself. "What? I'm accusing her? She accused me! I called her on her bullshit. I told her to tell you the truth, tell you what she really is – a swindler and a shyster."

"What a nerve!" Cassie moved back in and pushed him against the wall. "Tara, you can't trust this man. Do you know why he is being nice to you? Do you? It's because of a bet that he can get you into bed like the big boss man Leo. He's making a fool of you, isn't that right, Barry?"

Tara couldn't speak.

"No, Tara, that's not true. This has nothing to do—"

"I overheard them in the toilet," Cassie continued. "Plastic bitches talking about why he was interested in you and saying terrible things about you. Yes, I sorted that Joan bitch out. Nobody talks about my sister like that."

Tara put her hands over her ears. "Stop!"

"Tara, listen to me," Barry begged. "I never made any bet;

I don't know what she's talking about. She's making this up so you won't believe what I'm saying and she can take you for a ride. She's a fraudster and a con-artist and you should kick her out."

"I'm the con-artist? What a nerve. No, Tara, he's lying to you because I'm on to him. Did he show any interest in you before that Leo got you into bed?"

Tara shut her eyes, trying to block out the words. "Please go. Go now."

Barry smirked. "Yes, Cassie, or whoever you are, your time here has come to an end. Leave and crawl under whatever rock it was that you came from. Find another victim to manipulate."

Tara opened her eyes. "No, not Cassie, you Barry. You need to leave."

Barry threw his hands to the sky. "But, Tara, this woman is manipulating you. Can't you see? She is taking advantage. She's wormed her way into your life and your mother's life and you know absolutely nothing about her and, to top it all, she's accusing me of taking sordid bets and making a pass at you. You can't—"

"Shut up, shut up, shut up," Tara screamed. "Get out."

"Fine, I'm going!" Barry said, whisking his coat from a kitchen stool and slamming the door behind him. Tara fell into the couch and put her head in her hands. It was spinning with alcohol and accusations.

Cassie put her arm around her. "Thank you for taking my side. That never happens, but I promise you won't regret it."

Tara wiped away tears and attempted a laugh. "I'm kind of glad you beat Joan up, she's a rotten cow. But Barry – I thought he was nice. Do you really think he was after me for one thing, because of a *bet*?"

Cassie pulled her in so tight it felt like home. "It doesn't matter now. All that matters is that we have each other."

27

CASSIE

Friday, 25 November

Cassie passed the cabin-sized suitcase they'd shopped for together to Tara and ushered her out the door. "I will look after Mary; I promise. Now, go have fun!"

After last night's drama, she was exhausted but wanted to make sure Tara, who'd started her day with two paracetamols, didn't fall at the final hurdle.

Tara hesitated. "I don't think I'll go. Mother needs me and it's too much to put on you. Plus, I don't want to see Barry ever again."

Cassie reassured her all would be fine, that it was the hangover fear talking – something she knew from experience. If there were any problems, anything at all, she'd call.

Tara sighed. "If Sooty comes back, will you let me know?"

"He's fine," Cassie replied. "He's a cat. They come back."

With Tara gone, Cassie set about packing a bag for her week with Mary. Seven undisturbed nights with the old woman was exactly what she needed. Mary didn't tell Tara the good news about her health, which made Cassie wonder if it was news, or if it was something Mary knew all along – that she had more time than she was letting on. Was she dying at all? That day in the pizza place, where Tara was given the wrong pizza and wasn't sick, had got Cassie thinking. Something didn't add up. Perhaps it was nothing, but she already knew Mary wasn't the sweet, innocent old lady she pretended to be. She replayed the conversation about Mary's diagnosis with Tara in her mind – didn't Tara say she was at the party the night before Mary received the bad news and that she wished she'd been there for her?

Cassie got to work, cleaning up. Tara's apartment was so much nicer than when she came first, and Tara seemed to enjoy having her around. She loved being here. Of course, it would be great to have a house of her own, but it looked like that wouldn't happen as soon as she expected unless Mary took a turn for the worse.

After midday, Cassie set the security alarm on the apartment, locked up and left for Mary's. She promised Tara she would check back in on the place over the week, but it was a gated complex, nice and secure. It would be fine.

She let herself in to Mary's house, her home for the next week, and filled the kettle over the sink full of dirty dishes. The white and ginger cat came meowing and rubbed against her legs, but there was no sign of the old woman. She knocked on the bedroom door. "Mary, it's Joan. Can I get you a cup of tea?"

No answer. She pushed the door open slightly and Snowy squeezed out. "Are you okay, Mary?"

She peeped in to see the old lady lying in the bed. "Oh, hello dear. I'm so sorry, what time is it?"

Cassie opened the floral curtains and the light flooded in. "Don't apologise at all, Mary. It's not even one o'clock."

Mary gasped and tried to sit up. "What? One o'clock in the afternoon? Oh my word, how did I sleep so long? I never sleep past 8 a.m."

Cassie helped her into a sitting position. "How about I make you some tea and toast and you relax while I give the place a bloody good clean up. All the places you can't reach, what do you think?"

Mary patted around for her glasses and Cassie handed them to her. "Eh, okay, love. That would be great. Can you get me a glass of water for my tablets, too?"

"Of course, I will. Tara's gone off to work with her case packed, delighted with herself."

"Oh. Is she going today? I'm so confused. What day is it?"

"It's Friday, Mary, now relax and I'll be back to you in two shakes of a lamb's tail."

In the kitchen, Cassie cut the buttered toast into triangles, made a cup of black tea and carried it into the room where Mary was asleep again. It was almost a shame to wake the old lady, when she looked so peaceful, but she needed to eat. The last thing she wanted was for Tara to call and Mary say she didn't feel well. She'd never get out of Dublin airport then. Once 9 p.m. came and Tara was on that plane, Cassie could relax.

Mary nibbled the toast. "You're very good for coming, but you don't have to stay here all day; you can go out and about.

I'm well able to look after myself, although I don't feel great, if I'm honest."

Cassie gathered the clothes from the wooden chair in the corner. "Nonsense, I'm delighted to be here. You probably caught a virus off one of us, that's why you've been asleep for so long. Now it's best to rest and wait for it to pass."

Mary nodded. "That's probably it alright, a virus. They were saying on the news last night that the emergency services are out the door with this respiratory illness, did you see it?"

Cassie laughed. "Sure, didn't I watch the news here with you, Mary?"

Mary rubbed her head. "Did you? Oh, that's right, Joan, you did."

The Accident and Emergency crisis was on the news the night before. Hospitals all around the country packed with people on trolleys, chairs and even the floor. A trio of winter viruses were to blame, according to the suited newsreader.

"Better rest. You don't want to be landing into A&E now, do you? I'll tell you what, Mary, I'll leave you to your tea while I give the place a deep clean. Floors, high cupboards, that sort of thing. Will I put the TV on for you?"

"Uhm – yes please, love."

Cassie switched on the TV, where the lunchtime news and weather was well underway. She'd had enough news and weather in the last few weeks to do her a lifetime.

Now we cross over to Aoife Moore.

Thanks, Peter. Families have had a huge breakthrough in the Cherish the Child case, as the high court has ordered all remaining records to be made available to families.

"This is huge. It will allow us to see what happened to our

brothers and sisters who entered the convent and access our orig-
inal birth certs," a woman said.

Another woman appeared on screen.

"It's a good news day, but spare a moment for the parents who
gave up their children and, indeed, the parents who adopted them
who don't want their names revealed. They did what they were
told and now their lives will unravel. This isn't as straightforward
as it seems."

Cassie stood in the doorway and watched Mary's face for
any reaction, of which there was none. She couldn't help
herself. "I feel sorry for the kids," she said. "Imagine finding
out your whole life was a lie."

Mary regarded her for a moment before putting her cup
down with a shaky hand. She seemed to be waking up. "Different times, love. If the nuns told you to say nothing you
said nothing, you didn't question. You can't compare what
you see today with what we saw. A woman had two options:
become a nun or get married and have children, in that
order. Have you any yourself?"

Cassie jolted, surprised at the clarity of the question.
"Any children? Uhm, no. I never met someone special
enough to want to settle down with and, as for children, that
ship has sailed for me now."

Mary's face lit up. "You'd have loved my Frank; he was a
great man. Taken too soon. He called me his little buttercup,
on account of my blonde hair. He was such a good father,
too."

"Did you never have more children yourself, Mary?"

She smiled. "Children? No, just the one ..."

Cassie bit her lip.

"Of course, we wanted a football team, but we were
blessed with the one, that was our lot. We would have loved

more, but Tara was the best thing that ever happened to us."

"You know what?" Cassie clapped her hands. "I'll go down to the shop first and pick up something nice for us after dinner. Have a day off cooking, what do you say?"

"Come here for a minute," Mary said and patted the bed. Cassie sat down and Mary took her hand. "You're a good friend to Tara and a good person. I can feel it."

Cassie laughed her off. "Go on out of that, bet you say that to all the girls."

Across the road, at the 24/7, Cassie filled her basket with basic items - milk, bread, bananas and eggs. The self-service checkout was still broken and she queued right beside the saloon doors. Jeez, even in a tiny shop they had the alcohol section, but this time it didn't bother her. No thanks, she thought, and stepped forward when the shop assistant called the next customer. It was the young shop assistant from the other night.

"You must never go home," she joked with him and he smiled.

"I take all the shifts I can get. Need the money for college."

"Good for you," she said. "What are you studying?"

"Computer science. Final year. A few more months and I'll be out of here for good. Sorry, do I know you?"

"I came in the other night with my sis – my friend. She comes in here most evenings."

"Ah yes, now I remember. The two bottles a night woman."

"Excuse me?"

"She buys two bottles a night and ... and now I'm thinking I shouldn't have said that."

A man coughed behind Cassie, signalling her socially acceptable time at the checkout was up. And so was the conversation with the college student.

Back at Mary's house, Cassie let herself back in and set about putting the food away. Mary was back asleep, the white cat splayed at her feet, so she closed her bedroom door, then opened all the remaining downstairs windows, letting the fresh, albeit glacial, air rush in.

First, the litter trays. She cleaned them out, gagging at the stench of the urine-soaked clumps and replaced them with fresh woodchip. The air was freezing, but all that urea couldn't be good for your lungs.

Then she set about sweeping the floors. She tiptoed around Mary's bed and swept, pushing the wheelchair outside the bedroom door, then mopped the wooden floor. The water turned black with the dirt; by right Tara should be doing that job all the time.

With the house clean, and Mary still sleeping, she made a cup of coffee and flicked around the channels. She'd have to wake Mary up soon; Tara would surely phone to say goodbye before leaving and she didn't want her worrying about her mother's health. She wanted Tara to go to London and forget all about her mother.

28

TARA

Tara felt like a globetrotter on the train that morning, with her wheelie case, but she was dreading seeing Barry.

Spending the week with him was going to be hard. Trying to sleep with her for a bet and then saying all those things about Cassie was horrible, but that wasn't her main concern. If her mother passed away when she was gone, she'd never forgive herself.

"It's only London," Cassie had reassured her. "There are flights every hour. If anything happens, I will call, I promise."

She passed Joan in the walkway. "Have a good trip," she said and Tara nearly fell over. She put her head down passing Barry's office; he was the last person she wanted to see. Luckily, his blinds were closed.

The flight wasn't until 9:10 p.m. The group taxi was booked for 5:30 p.m. to allow for Friday traffic and the inevitable airport security tailbacks, but she really didn't want to travel with Barry. She rang and booked her own taxi for 4:30 p.m. instead and sent an email to let her fellow travellers know. She could have a few drinks in the airport first.

"Tara, can I speak to you for a few minutes?"

It was Barry. Damn it.

She didn't turn around. "I'd rather not, thank you."

"It wasn't a request. My office. Now."

John whistled in a "you're in trouble" tone. She couldn't wait until she moved to her new office and away from his smug face. Barry stomped into his office and slammed his door shut. She followed him in.

"Right, I am going to say this once and let it be done then," he said and paced the floor. "I stayed quiet once before when I shouldn't have, and I regret it to this day. What happened between you and Leo was wrong, very wrong. There – I said it. People were there that night, people saw him bring you to the room, they knew you were drunk and they did nothing. I wasn't there, but I heard after. It was me that reported it to HR, but I did it anonymously because I was worried for my job. That was weak and wrong of me."

"The party was my fault. I had too much to drink," Tara said. "It was my fault."

"No. No, it wasn't." Barry rubbed his neck. "Tara, I don't know what happened between you two, but you were very drunk and he brought you to a room, a man in a very senior position. Now, here's the truth. Cards on the table. The reason I persuaded you to go for the customer liaison manager job is because day after day, for the last God knows how long, you come in on time, you work and you leave not a minute early. Yet, time after time, I see people being promoted ahead of you. Christ, even I came in after you and now I'm your manager. That's not right!"

Tara felt the heat start at her chest and flush her whole face. Her neck was drenched and, while she wished he'd stop, the determination in his eyes told her he was far from finished. He paced again.

"You deserve a break, and yes, I like you. Is that a crime? Not for what I can get, and definitely *not* for a bet, wherever that rumour started. Now, let's be clear – I'm not making advances on you. It's against company policy to date a subordinate, as you know. Jeez, you could have taken that bastard to the cleaners."

"I didn't want—"

He held out his hands. "Let me finish because this is important, and if I don't keep going I might lose my nerve. I like you, Tara, and when the promotion came up, yes, I admit I was thinking selfishly. I was thinking of myself because I could ask you out if you moved to another department. You're different – there's no bullshit with you, not like, well, everyone else in this department, out for their own gains. You are happy to come in, do your work and you always shoot from the hip, no matter what it means for you."

Tara didn't know what to say.

"Which now brings me to the reason I brought you in here today. That woman Cassie, she's dangerous. I have been around people like her before and, I tell you, she is. I kept my mouth shut before and I won't again. She attacked Joan in the bathroom and then attacked me. You've taken her into your home and are giving her unsupervised access to your ailing mother for a week. Tara, this is not a good idea. Please listen to me."

"But she's my sister. I have proof and, besides, I'm all booked for the week. Flights, hotel, transfers, training. They're expecting me and I have to go."

He plonked into his chair. "What exactly do you know about this woman?"

"Like what?"

"Where was she before she moved in with you?"

"Uhm, homeless."

"Before that. Where was she living before becoming homeless?"

Cassie didn't talk much about where she was before, and the realisation sent a shiver down Tara's spine. Then she remembered. "She said she was in a woman's shelter in Mayo run by a celebrity."

"Women's refuge ..." Barry typed on his keyboard. "Celebrity ... Mayo. Aha! Found you." He jumped up and grabbed his coat, then opened the door. "Come on."

"Uhm, what? Where?"

"To Mayo." He checked his watch. "I'll drive. There's one refuge registered for the county and there's a phone number. They probably won't speak to us, but it's got to be worth a try. If we hurry, we'll ask a few questions and get back in time for the flight. That's if they check out. If not, what you do is up to you, but at least you'll know. No, at least I will know that this time I did the right thing."

Tara didn't move.

"Are you coming?" he asked.

"Why should I trust you? Why should I believe you over Cassie?"

He sighed deeply. "Because I know I am right. Please, trust me. Please."

Tara thought of her mother in the wheelchair, with nobody else to check on her. She didn't have a choice. "We can't just vanish from here without telling anyone."

"Okay," Barry said, then disappeared for a moment before returning. "I've told the others we'll meet them at the airport. Now, are you coming or not?"

29

TARA

It took two hours, a lot of it spent on bad roads, to reach the west coast. Dignity House was beautiful, not at all what Tara expected from a refuge. An old estate house at the top of a long gravel driveway, with rolling green fields on one side and the open ocean on the other. Barry pulled his blue Ford Focus around the back of the house, as directed by a large woman in glasses.

Tara had called ahead and asked if she could visit, but didn't say why. Barry reckoned they were more likely to get information that way. Apart from the grating voice of Google Maps and the detailed account of Barry's new car, the journey down was pleasant. They stopped for coffee and Barry was good company, sometimes speaking and other times quiet. A few times he made her laugh, with croissant crumbs on his lips that he didn't know about, but his jumper draped over his open-necked shirt made her want to laugh the loudest. He looked like a doctor. If this had been any other journey in any other circumstances, it would have been fun, but it was almost midday and the clock was ticking.

"Tara, is it?" the woman asked and Tara nodded. "I'm Sharon, we spoke on the phone earlier. You're very welcome to Dignity House. Come in out of the cold." She turned to Barry. "You're welcome to wait in the conservatory. I've left some newspapers and there's some tea and coffee. Make yourself comfortable."

Barry bit his lip. "I was hoping to come in with Tara."

Sharon's smile didn't falter. "I'm sorry but that's not possible. It's nothing personal but this is a safe place for women and children and only pre-approved workers are allowed in."

Barry looked like a little boy scolded.

Sharon put her hand on his arm. "You understand, I'm sure."

He didn't look happy but agreed, and Tara followed Sharon into the house, down a hallway and into an office, where she closed the mahogany door behind them. She invited Tara to take a seat in the high-roofed room and she sat herself in a large black leather chair. "So, what can we do you for? How can I be of help?"

"I'm looking for information on someone who stayed here. My sister, Cassie Blake?"

Sharon's eyes widened. "Cassie Blake is your sister?"

"Yes. My big sister. We met for the first time a few weeks ago, through a DNA site. She's been staying with me in Dublin since, but I don't really know anything about her. She said she was here for a while and I was hoping you could give me some information on her."

Sharon's demeanour changed. "I'm sorry you came so far.

Dublin, wasn't it? Yes, Dublin. It's a pity you didn't tell me this on the phone. I'd have told you not to come. It's unethical for me to tell you anything about anyone who may," she paused, "or may not have stayed here. Have you tried talking to her first?"

"But you know her. When I said her name, you knew her."

Sharon rearranged pencils on her desk. "Tara, you must understand. This is a woman's refuge. Many of our residents have come from dangerous situations. We can't possibly give out information on them." She stood and opened the door. "I'm truly sorry I wasted your time and I wish you luck in the future."

Tara followed her back through the kitchen, where a little girl was standing on a stool beside a flour-covered table as a woman cut Christmas tree shapes from pastry. Tara's heart panged. Cassie never knew their mother and here she was trying to find dirt on her behind her back. She caught up with Sharon, as she crossed the courtyard.

"Sharon, please. Cassie told me she stayed here; I know she did. I just want to know what she was like – was she good, bad, sad ... anything you can tell me."

Barry came out of the conservatory. "Any joy?"

Sharon shook her head. "I'm sorry. I'm bound by confidentiality."

He looked all around him. "Lovely place you have here."

Sharon smiled. "It is, isn't it? We are very proud of the women here. They are remarkable, many overcoming massive obstacles. We're very lucky to have this as a home for them."

Tara didn't see how Barry could be so calm, having driven all this way for nothing. She wasn't giving up. "I live on my own and my mother is elderly, and I need to know what kind of person Cassie is because she is minding my mother right now. Surely you can tell me if she's a good person or a bad person. That's all I need to know."

"Tara, leave it. She said she is bound by confidentiality," Barry said, heading to the car. "Thanks for your time, Sharon."

Sharon crossed her arms and stood watching.

Barry rolled down his window. "We're going to stop off for lunch. Is there somewhere you'd recommend that we might get something satisfying? We don't mind travelling, if it's worth it."

Sharon stared at him and he stared back. Finally, she glanced at the ground. "Lenburgh is nice at this time of year. There's a nice little place beside the post office."

Barry started the engine and Sharon stood back to let them past. He drove up the driveway.

"Well, that was a waste of time and petrol," Tara said. "She couldn't tell me anything, not a single thing. What do we do now?"

At the end of the driveway, where the grounds met the main road, Barry indicated left instead of right.

"Where are you going?" Tara asked. "This isn't the way to Dublin."

He smiled and put his sunglasses on. "To find out about your sister."

Lenburgh was a small village with a post office, a little café, a church, a grocery store and seven pubs. Barry pulled into a parking spot outside the post office, his car the only one on the road.

"I'm lost. What is happening?" Tara asked.

"Sharon recommended this place when I asked for something satisfying. Now, I could be wrong, but I think she was trying to tell us to come here because she said the café beside the post office and ..."

Tara looked out her window. There was no café.

"I think she was giving us some important information," he said.

People never ceased to confound Tara. She had got none of that from their exchange, but Barry tapped his head. "Up there for thinking," he said. "Let's see if anyone in here knows anything about Cassie. Have you a photo?"

Tara flicked through her phone and found the two of them. "I like this one. It's from the night of your birthday."

He diverted his gaze. "You looked really gorgeous that night."

A bell tinkled as they entered the empty post office, where a tiny, white-haired woman was stamping parcels in the back.

"I'll be with you in a minute," she called out, her voice small and croaky.

"Take your time," Barry called back. He put his sunglasses into his top pocket as the old lady walked at turtle-speed to the counter.

"How may I help you?"

"Hi," he said. "How are you doing? Listen, we were in the area, and hoping to speak to a friend. We think she may have lived around here, but we didn't get her address. Maybe you could help us out?"

The old woman narrowed her eyes. "Have you a name?"

"Cassie Blake. We have a picture. Tara?"

Tara showed the picture to the lady, who peered over her glasses. She did a double-take.

"How did you say you know this woman?" the post-mistress asked.

"She's an acquaintance," Barry said. "If there's anything you can tell us about her at all, like is she trustworthy, is she reliable, we'd be most grateful."

"Trustworthy? Trustworthy?" the old lady almost snarled. "Are you joking? This woman is the lowest of the low. She should be locked up and the key thrown away."

Tara was well clued in what was going on this time. "Please tell me. I need to know. Whatever it is, please."

The old lady tensed. "That woman is scum. Came from scum, grew up as scum, a liar and a thief. Poor Mrs Graham, God rest her soul, didn't deserve it. She didn't deserve to go like that. After all she did for her. Scum."

Mrs Graham – that name rang a bell.

"I warned Mrs Graham to get rid of her, but would she listen? Not at all. Even though her health degenerated and she was coming in here less and less. That woman was even collecting her pension for her, which I knew wasn't right at the time. I said it. I called up to the house to see her, but that woman wouldn't let me in. People talk, you know, especially in small towns like this. They said she was trying to get Mrs Graham to sign over her house to her on account of her daughter Kimberley living abroad, then the daughter comes home to find her fears are founded – her mother has signed the house away. She fights for it and wins and next of all her mother is dead."

She tutted and blessed herself.

Barry searched on his phone. "I can't find any mention of this in the news."

The old woman smiled. "No, and you won't either because she's an evil, conniving so-and-so. I believe it was in her from when she was child, tortured a poor defenceless kitten. Little girls don't do things like that. Mrs Graham's death was considered natural, of course it was, but every last person in this town knows the truth."

It was then that Tara remembered how she knew the name. "Wait ... Mrs Graham. Is that the woman who took Cassie in when she was small?"

The lady leaned forward, relishing the gossip, however horrible. "The very one."

The door swung open and a man in a flat cap and mac came in, shuffling with the aid of a walking stick.

"I'll be with you now, Donal." She scribbled a note and passed it to Tara under the reinforced glass screen.

"That's the address of Mrs Graham's homeplace. I hear Kimberley is home from New York, packing up the last few things for storage before the new owners move in. She'll tell you what you need to know first-hand."

AFTER THREE WRONG turns and a white-knuckle twenty-minute drive through the tightest roads, they found Clover House simply because there was a removal van parked in the driveway.

Tara had wanted to go straight back to Dublin and rescue her mother, but Barry persuaded her to finish what they had started. He picked up a chicken fillet roll and a cup of tea from the deli across the road before they left Lenburgh, but she couldn't find anything suitable to eat so made do with a black coffee. Her stomach rumbled as Barry drove along the coast, but there was no time to lose.

At the house, a glamorous woman with what looked like a lot of plastic surgery was giving orders to two men in overalls carrying a sofa from the house. She stopped when she saw them. "Can I help you?" She had an American accent.

"I'm looking for Kimberley Graham?"

"You found her – lucky you. How can I help?"

"Can we go inside? It's sensitive."

Kimberley bit her lip before nodding. "Sure, but I don't have long. I have a million things to do before flying back home in the morning."

Inside the bare walls of the kitchen, they stood. "Sorry I can't offer you a beverage or a seat, I'm getting the last of Mom's things ready for auction before heading back to New York. What can I do for you?"

Tara said nothing, but pulled out her phone and showed her the picture of Cassie.

Kimberley recoiled. "Who are you? What do you want?"

"No, please don't worry, we're just trying to find out about her, that's all. We hear she stayed here as a child and then again recently."

Kimberley leaned against the kitchen counter for support, breathing heavily. "Forgive me, but I hate that woman with every fibre of my being."

"Please," Barry said. "What happened?"

She took a deep breath. "My mother was the sweetest person you could meet and took her in as a child. Cassie Blake. She was four and I was seven. Daddy told Mom not to, warned she'd be too damaged from living in care, but she wouldn't listen. Thought she could give her a good life but didn't realise the monster she was welcoming into our home. She put us all through hell for six months. In the end, when" – she took a breath – "when she mutilated my cat, she had to go back. I thought that was the last we'd see of her, but years later she crawls back under a different name. Says she's a carer and moves in while I'm abroad. Next thing you know, Mom is dead."

Tara couldn't believe her ears. "No. Cassie wouldn't hurt a fly," she insisted, but already her mind was with Sooty and how he had disappeared the only night Cassie was there alone.

Just then, Kimberley's phone rang. "I need to take this. If you have any sense, run as far away from that dangerous bitch as you can," she said and hurried outside to take the call.

"Tara," Barry said. "Are you okay?"

"No, I'm not. Why would she say all those things?"

Barry tilted his head. "Maybe because it's true. Let's go."

As they drove back through the stone-walled narrow roads, Tara's head was spinning.

"I knew she was a fraud," Barry said. "We need to get to your mother."

"I need to talk to Cassie," Tara said, unlocking her phone, but Barry swiped it from her hand.

"No! Don't ring her! What if a fraction of what those two women said was true? We need to get your mother to safety without alerting Cassie. Get your mother out, then we can ask all the questions we like."

30

TARA

"Hi, Cassie, how's it all going there?" Tara made the call from the taxi. The main thing was to remain calm, not to alert Cassie that anything had changed. A lorry tooted its horn long and loud in the lane to their right, making her jump.

"Hi, hun, all's good here. Are you in traffic?"

"Yes, on the way to the airport now. Should be there by seven."

Tara watched as the lorry driver glanced in his rear-view mirror and blew out his cheeks in despair at them.

"I'm so excited for you," Cassie said. "Imagine, in a few hours you'll be in England! Have an absolute ball and don't worry about a thing here, we'll be grand. Can you believe you're actually going?"

"No! It's crazy but good crazy. Listen, where are you now?"

"In Mary's house, like we agreed, hun. Why?"

"Great. Could you do me a favour? I was going through the checklist of things I have to bring to training and I don't know how I missed it, but I forgot my iPad, and I don't want to get off on the wrong foot. I hate to ask you to do more when you're helping out so much already, but if you don't mind, could you get the iPad from my apartment and bring it to departures in Terminal 1? I won't have time to swing by before the flight."

The taxi came to a standstill in traffic again and Tara held her breath. Everything depended on the outcome of this question.

"Of course, hun, no problem," Cassie said, and Tara exhaled in pure relief. "Mary's asleep anyway, so I'll fly around by the apartment and get it."

Tara's stomach fell. "Mother is asleep at dinner time? Is she okay?"

Again, a pause. "Yeah, of course she is. She's having a little sleep, sure she might as well. Don't worry, she's eaten throughout the day and had plenty of cups of tea. I'll get her to call you later unless you want me to wake her up?"

Wake her up, let me talk to her, Tara wanted to scream. "No, leave her sleep," is what she said instead. "I'll be at the airport in about half an hour. Will you get there as soon as you can? Oh, and any sign of Sooty?" She held her breath.

"No sign, but sure he's a cat. He'll go off and sow his wild oats and come back when he's had enough. Don't worry! Now go on, I'll get the iPad and meet you there."

Tara ended the call and immediately dialled Barry, who was already in Dublin airport.

"She's on her way," Tara said. "The traffic is brutal."

"Excellent. I'll hang around here till she comes. Are you sure you don't want me to come with you? Because I will. I will ditch the flight, just say the word."

Tara didn't want that. Barry had a delegation of new

recruits waiting for him. They needed him and, besides, she wanted to do this herself, for once. It was her plan; she'd thought of it. It was her problem and she wanted to prove to herself that she could fix it. It was simple: get Cassie out, get in, get Mary out and to a safe place, then they could talk. Barry would stall Cassie at departures until Tara let him know Mary was out of the house. They agreed a safe word if under duress – by which they meant danger. If either Tara or Barry said that word, the other would call the police.

"Must have been a crash," the taxi driver said. "Rubber-neckers slowing down to look. Once we get past it, we'll fly along. Now, is it the airport or Cushla you want to go to?"

"Cushla," Tara said. "It's complicated."

"None of my business, love." The driver tutted. "I see it all and say nothing, but I will tell you this – it's a tangled web we weave, when first we practise to deceive. Shakespeare."

"Scott, actually," Tara muttered under her breath, as an image of her mother flashed through her mind, vulnerable and sleeping when, in her whole life, she had never missed dinner time.

"Sorry?" he said, but Tara was already ringing Barry back. He picked up. "What is it?"

She lowered her voice. "There's something terribly wrong, I can feel it. I'm going to call the police. What if she's already done something to Mother?"

"No, Tara, we talked about this. You call the guards and say what? Your sister is looking after your mother?"

"But—"

"And they take you seriously and call to the house. What will they find? An old lady with a woman she has invited into her home and who she wants to be there? No, Tara, get your mother out of there and then talk to Cassie. It's a good plan, have faith in yourself."

"Mother was asleep when I called and ... and ..." Tara's voice broke. "Sooty is still missing. He never goes missing."

"Tara, stop it! Cassie is on her way to the airport, where I'll stall her while you get Mary out of her house and to safety. Trust me, it will work!"

The taxi started and stopped again. Red and orange lights to their right and snaking in the longest line in front, as far as the eye could see. The rain battered the windscreen. "Oh God, this is awful. I wish this traffic would move quicker."

"Stay calm. You can do this."

Cars sped up the slip road, illuminating a huge road sign up ahead.

"Can you take the next left?" Tara asked the taxi driver, her vision beginning to swim. Oh no, not a migraine. She rummaged in her handbag to no avail. She'd forgotten to pack her medication.

"Do you have any painkillers?" she asked the taxi driver.

"Sorry, love, I used to, but we're not allowed give them out anymore. Against health regulations. Woke brigade gone mad, sure you can't do anything these days. Now, are you sure you want to take that slip road? Traffic could be worse that way, with it being Christmas and all."

The lights ahead danced and her stomach felt sick. "Please. I need to get home ASAP."

"You're the boss, love."

31

CASSIE

With the iPad in her backpack, Cassie caught a taxi and headed for the airport. This was the last thing she wanted to do, but, reading between the lines, Tara was getting cold feet and she didn't want her to change her mind.

The flight was at nine, almost two hours away, but the security delays at departures had been on the news for the last few nights and this was quite late for Tara to be leaving it to go through. The song playing on the car radio cut off as the taxi came to a sudden stop a few kilometres from the airport.

Breaking news coming in of an overturned lorry on the N1 between Drumcondra and Santry obstructing both lanes of traffic.

The driver turned up the sound.

Unconfirmed reports of at least one fatality. We'll keep you posted. In the meantime, consider using another route for your journey tonight, and keep safe.

The windscreen wipers swished back and forth as time

passed and Cassie's anxiety began to rise. She needed to get this iPad to Tara or she wouldn't be going anywhere. Now there were ninety minutes to her flight. She called Tara but her phone was busy. She texted her.

> Hey, traffic is crazy, a crash coming out of the city blocking both lanes. What is the queue like at security?

Two ticks. No answer.

She rang again. Nothing, and her stomach dropped. The crash was coming from Dublin city. What if it was Tara? She could barely breathe, gasping for breath. She couldn't stand the thoughts of losing her, having come so far. If she died, Cassie's world would fall apart. She called again, and when it rang out she powered up the iPad to find it screen locked with a four-digit code. She entered the passcode – the same as the alarm code on her apartment – her year of birth. People were so predictable, and Tara was no different, using their year of birth if single, or the year they married if they were a couple. The screen unlocked and she scrolled across through the apps, almost crying when she saw it. The Find My Phone app.

She entered Tara's number and a map filled the screen with the phone's location, the phone still powered on. She was almost afraid to look, as she zoomed in to find the phone was not on the N1 at Santry. Thank God. She watched as the little dot moved further away from the airport. What was Tara doing? Maybe she'd changed her mind.

Cassie called again and this time Tara picked up. "Hey, letting you know I'm on the way, see you in twenty."

"Great, thanks for that, see you there."

Cassie followed the dot with her finger towards Cushla

and Mary's house. Tara was lying. She wasn't going to the airport. She was going home.

Why was Tara lying to her, getting her to collect her iPad and bring it to the airport when she wasn't there herself? Unless ... she had found out?

"I need to get out of the car. Can you let me out here?" she said to the driver.

"No can do. It's a motorway. There's nowhere for you to go and it's illegal."

She threw a twenty-euro note at him and opened the back door of the taxi. "Sorry, it's an emergency. My mother isn't well."

"You nutcase," he shouted out the window. "You're dressed all in black on a bloody motorway, are you on a death wish?"

But Cassie was running and already through the three lanes of stationary traffic to the safety of the median and its shrubbery. A thick metal fence surrounded by thorny bushes was between her and the other side, where traffic was speeding from the city. Lorries and cars sped by on the 120km-limit road, oblivious to the woman in black at the centre. The sheer force of the traffic along with the noise startled her but, spotting a gap, she put her head down and sprinted across the road to the blare of car horns with one narrowly missing her as she dived onto the grass on the other side. Panting, she caught her breath then ran along the hard shoulder and up the next exit. Her lungs burnt and she gasped for breath as she ran up the slip road to the Airside industrial estate and hailed down a taxi.

"Please ... can ... you ... take ... me ... to Cushla. It's an emergency."

"Hop in," the taxi driver said. "I'll have you there in ten minutes."

32

TARA

The taxi stopped outside her mother's house and she got out in the throes of a migraine. She felt down to open the garden gate, her sight blotchy and her hands numb. The aura was bad, which meant the headache would be chronic. There were packs of paracetamol in her mother's medicine cabinet; they'd take the edge off until she could get her proper meds.

Barry would be meeting Cassie about now, which meant Tara had an hour max to get her mother out, if he successfully stalled her. It could be as little as twenty minutes if he didn't. No time to waste. She turned the key and let herself in.

"Mother, it's Tara," she called out.

"In here, love," Mary called back from her bedroom and Tara almost cried. She was alive. She closed her eyes for a moment and when she opened them black blotches appeared in her view but, even still, she could see that her mother did not look well. Her face was deathly pale and her lips were blue.

"Mother, we have to get you out of here for a bit, just for a little while. The erm ... gas is being checked and they asked us to leave."

Mary groaned. "No, love. I'm not feeling great. Tell them to come back another time." She turned over in the bed, away from Tara.

"No, Mother, we have to go. Come on, let's get you up out of bed and into your chair."

Tara tried to lift Mary but she grimaced. "No, I'm not going. I don't feel well. Where's Joan? And you were supposed to be going away. What's going on?"

"Please, Mother. I don't have time to explain, but Joan isn't who she said she is. Please just work with me."

She pulled Mary to a sitting position and went to get her wheelchair. It was gone.

"I don't feel so good," Mary said before vomiting all over the bed. The contents of Tara's stomach almost followed suit. She ran to the kitchen to get a basin from under the sink and a cloth to clean up, right beside the medicine box. Her hand touched a card of paracetamol. With the side of her head throbbing, she grabbed the paracetamol and turned on the cold tap. She reached into the press to get a glass, almost falling over the wheelchair in her way. What was that doing there? She took hold of it and swung it around. "Come on, Mother, we have to go before she gets back."

"Before who gets back?" a voice demanded.

Tara dropped the meds and screamed.

33

TARA

Tara fell backwards, flailing and screaming. "Please don't hurt us."

"Oh, for God's sake, Tara, get up off the floor and don't be so dramatic. What are you talking about?"

Tara pulled herself up from the floor and grabbed the biggest kitchen knife from the block on the counter. She waved it at Cassie. "Let us go or I will use this, I swear I will!"

Cassie laughed. "Will you stop it and sit down."

Tara panted, backing away from Cassie but still holding the knife. "I know you're an evil person who hurts people. I know who you are."

"Girls, is everything okay out there?" Mary called in a weak voice.

Tara glanced to the bedroom, then back to Cassie, knife in her hand. "No, Mother, it's not. Call the police."

Cassie laughed hard. "Great idea! Call the police, Mary, please do. Be my guest."

"Is that you, Joan?" Mary called out.

"Her name is Cassie, Mother," Tara replied, "not Joan,

and she's leaving now." She lowered her voice. "I know what you did to Mrs Graham. I know."

Cassie gasped. "Don't you dare say I did anything to that woman."

"I know you hurt her and it seems everyone in Lenburgh knows about it too. We went there today, me and Barry, and we found out all about you."

"Really. All about me, or what everyone told you about me? I never touched Mrs Graham; I loved Mrs Graham. She was like a mother to me."

"I met Kimberley and I heard what you did to the cat. That's evil. You're a psychopath. What did you do with Sooty? Did you kill him, because if you did, I swear—"

Cassie slammed her fist on the table. "Jesus Christ, will you stop! I didn't kill Mrs Graham and I never harmed any cat. All my damn life I have had to take this, being the fall guy, being blamed for everything that went wrong. That one is out for herself, that one is evil. Blah blah blah."

Tara faltered. "But Kimberley's kitten ..."

"Kimberley Graham was a self-centred little bitch. It was the reason her mother brought me into their home in the first place, to get a friend for her, to see if it would help with her 'worrying' traits. Her father thought the sun shone out of her backside, but Mrs Graham, she knew what Kimberley was. In the six months I was there, that child terrorised me. It is rare you will meet a psychopath in life, but she was one. After six months of Kimberley torturing her own cat to blame on me, Mrs Graham knew there was no hope for her daughter and returned me to the orphanage for my own safety, and I was bloody glad. Imagine being glad to go back there – well, I was, because while there was badness in CTC, nothing came close to the pure evil of their darling Kimberley. It was easier to tell the neighbours I was to blame for the horrors than to face reality. Blood is thicker than water."

"But the old woman in the post office said you isolated Mrs Graham, then killed her to get her house. She said everybody knows that."

"Ah, Mrs O'Leary, what a windbag. Mrs Graham died of natural causes. When Kimberley came back, sniffing for money and land, she was afraid of her. Imagine that, afraid of her own daughter! Kimberly tried to visit but I'd seen enough of what she could do and I loved that old woman. I loved her like a mother and there was no way Kimberley was getting near her. She nearly freaked when she heard Mrs Graham had signed her beloved cottage over to me; it was the final gut punch to her. Mrs Graham knew her darling daughter would sell it, even though it had been the family home for generations. Armed with lawyers, she claimed her mother wasn't of sound mind and got them to retract the changes to the will. A week later Kimberley put it up for sale, despite her mother's wishes. As I say, a self-centred, evil bitch."

Tara was standing open-mouthed. "You're lying. They said you'd do that. Lie. Let us go."

"People only see what they want to see. What happened with Mrs Graham was not like that. Not even close, and what do you mean let you go?" Cassie held her hands out. "Tara, you're the one with the knife."

34

CASSIE

Three years previously

I t was quite the coincidence when Cassie saw the advertisement online.

Wanted: Live-in clean non-smoker required to care for elderly lady as daughter moving abroad. Bed, board and generous living allowance provided. Please call after 6 p.m.

Cassie poured herself a drink. She'd been dabbling – nothing serious – but two weeks ago her landlord told her he was selling up and she had six weeks to vacate. The problem was she was on social welfare, and with the economy booming, finding somewhere to live on her rent allowance was impossible.

Until last year, that allowance would have got her a

decent one-bedroom flat in town, but the lowest rent she could find now was €100 above her limit, and crowds of desperate renters queued for them on open days. Economists warned of a boom-bust and she hoped the bust would come soon because nobody wanted to give her a job in this town and there was no boom on the dole.

Cassie wasn't unemployable. She was reliable, a hard worker and trustworthy – when she was sober. She'd tried rehab a couple of times, but it never worked for her, and it seemed easier to stop letting people down, roll her own cigarettes and buy cheap wine. She could handle letting herself down, she'd done it all her life. Besides, she had good company.

She tore a phone number from the page and called the number. It was answered immediately. An American woman snapped that she was the daughter in question and to come for interview at 6 p.m. if she could make it.

"Have you a pen and I will give you the address?" the woman asked.

Cassie mimed writing with a pen to the assistant at customer service and she handed her one from her white shirt, then Cassie was turning over the paper with the phone number on and scribbling down the address.

"Clover House, Lenburgh." Cassie stopped still. Clover House. Surely it wasn't Mrs Graham? She had visited Cassie every week when she was in CTC as promised, but they had lost contact over the years, mostly because Cassie couldn't stand to see the pain in her eyes when she screwed up yet again. She'd heard that Mr Graham had died a few years back and had meant to go to the funeral, but she couldn't bring herself to. He'd let Cassie take the blame for the cat, even though it was him that caught Kimberley with it in the shed. He put his head in the sand and blamed Cassie for everything because, as Cassie knew now, he was afraid of his own daughter. She didn't care; he was an adult and she was a vulnerable child. It didn't matter how uncomfortable it was, he should have told the truth. No, he didn't deserve her presence at his funeral.

"Are you still there?" the woman asked.

Cassie gathered herself. "I'll be there. Who should I ask for?"

"Ask for me. Kimberley Graham. I'm her daughter."

Mrs Graham recognised Cassie straight away, but when Kimberley was talking to another woman with a tight bun and navy skirt suit, she leaned into Cassie. "You're drinking again, aren't you?"

Cassie couldn't lie to her. "Yes, just a little though."

"If I hire you, will you be able to keep yourself on the straight and narrow?"

"Absolutely." Cassie nodded. "I swear you won't have a worry about me, but what about Kimberley?"

Mrs Graham winked at Cassie. "She's off to America, wanted to put me in a home and sell this place from under me. You leave her to me."

Kimberley shook the other woman's hand and took a paper file from her before joining Cassie and Mrs Graham. "You two look cosy," she said, her voice strained and aloof. "Do you know each other?" She cocked her head and squinted at Cassie. "Sorry, you seem familiar. Have we met?"

Cassie breathed deeply to try to slow her racing heart. "No, I don't think so. It's Alison. Alison Byrne. Pleased to meet you."

Mrs Graham grinned. "She's a lovely girl."

"Have you references?" Kimberley asked.

"She's going to get them, aren't you?" Mrs Graham said, then beckoned her daughter to her. "She's got the first aid and the FETAC 5, and she's nice. I want her to mind me."

Kimberley looked her up and down. "Maybe we'll do a trial run."

"Maybe we won't," Mrs Graham said. "It's my life. Now tell the others to go, this is the woman I'm hiring."

Kimberley didn't look happy as she ushered the others out. Mrs Graham whispered to Cassie, "I'm tired of her telling me what to do with my life. I want you and that's final. Can you start on Monday?"

With Kimberley gone and just the two of them there, it was the happiest Cassie had ever been. Mrs Graham was like a mother to her and caring for her was no inconvenience whatsoever. She even managed to cut out on the alcohol, and Mrs Graham turned a blind eye to the smoking.

Two years she was there, when the old woman called her into her bedroom. She'd been getting weaker and Cassie was afraid. Afraid that Mrs Graham's time was coming close.

Cassie loved the peace and serenity with just the two of them. The house had been in the Graham family for generations and the wild garden was the perfect place to sit whiling away the hours, chatting and pondering. Mrs Graham got slower and slept longer until she stopped going outside at all.

"Sit down there and give me my glasses, love, will you?" she asked one day when Cassie brought her the files she requested.

"Now," she said, "I'm no fool. I know my time is almost here. I've had a good life, and I'm ready to go, but there's a few things I need you to help me with first."

Cassie fought back the tears. What she was saying was heart-breaking but also true.

"Now, dear," the old lady said. "Chances are you've been calling Kimberley to come home, but she's not here, so we can assume that hasn't made a difference."

Cassie didn't say anything.

"It doesn't surprise me, although I thought with the mention of death she'd be back to see me off and have this place sold before I'm even cold."

"Don't say that, she's your daughter. Remember you told me, blood is thicker than water?"

Mrs Graham took her glasses off and rubbed her eyes. "I'm sorry, Cassie. I'm sorry I didn't fight harder for you. You were a child, you had nobody. Mr Graham, he was afraid to face the truth about his darling daughter, but I should have made him see. I'm truly sorry and, to show I am, I'm leaving it to you on one condition."

"Leaving what?"

"Clover House, of course. You're the only one who's cared for me for the last two years. The only visitor, the only caller ... nobody else gave a continental about me, but you did. Cassie, I love you as a daughter and you deserve some kindness, something to call your own. You love this place like I do, don't you?"

Cassie nodded. "You know I do, but I couldn't possibly—"

"And you would never sell it?"

"Never."

"Give me the pen."

"No, this is crazy."

"No, it's not. It is my house and I will leave it to who I

like." She signed her name and handed the document to Cassie. "It's yours."

———

A MONTH later Cassie's heart broke for the second time in her life when Mrs Graham died peacefully in her bed. The next day Kimberley came home, spitting all sorts of accusations when she discovered it was Cassie who had cared for her mother. Deception, coercion, murder. A team of lawyers landed and, at the reading of the will, Kimberley got nothing. Then the rumours spread. Mrs Graham was senile. She was coerced into signing over the house by the fraudster Cassie Blake, the same one as she'd fostered as a child. It was claimed she'd alienated the old lady from her friends and especially her doting daughter Kimberley, who'd tried to make contact but was cut off and had no idea her mother was dying. Then she pulled out the big guns. This so-called carer was a child of Cherish the Child, a damaged lowlife, the very same girl who had once tortured and killed her cat.

The whole town believed it, every last one of them. Cassie found herself on the street with nowhere to go and nobody to care what became of her, ostracised in the community. The two litres of vodka and pills should have ended her pain for good, but someone found her that night, in the alleyway, tucked away from the shoppers on the main street.

That someone then called an ambulance and insisted on travelling with her, staying until she woke up. That someone was Sharon, the manager at Dignity House.

35

TARA

Friday, 25 November

Tara's head was banging and her hand that held the knife had gone completely numb. She felt like she was going to puke. "I need to take medication for my headache."

"Take it, I'm not stopping you."

She picked up two tablets with trembling hands, filled a glass from the draining board with water and knocked them back. All this was too confusing, making her headache worse. A black cat jumped up onto the window ledge outside. Sooty.

"Why didn't you tell me?" Tara asked. "When you came to stay with me, you never told me any of this."

"Because I knew what you would think, the same as everyone else, that's why, and look at you now, tricking me to get me out of the house. See, I knew this would happen, but

I did nothing wrong and I wouldn't ever do anything to you. You're my sister."

Tara thought about the DNA test and how that was all she had to prove their relationship. "Are you, though? Are you my sister?"

"Of course, I am. Haven't we got proof?"

"What's happening out there?" Mary called.

"I think it's time we asked Mother what happened," Tara said. "Once and for all. I think it's time we found out the truth."

CASSIE FOLLOWED Tara into the bedroom where the ginger cat sniffed at the vomit on Mary's floral duvet. She was sitting up in the bed, her face a strange shade of grey.

"Tara, put down that knife like a good girl," Mary said, and Tara lay it on the chest of drawers beside her but still within arm's reach. "What's going on?"

Tara took her mother's hand and rubbed it. "I'm not cross with you, and I don't want you to be upset, Mother, but we haven't been honest with you. This isn't Joan. Her name is Cassie, and she claims to be my sister."

Mary gasped. "What? No, no, you have no sister. It's just you."

"Mary, we know," Cassie said. "We have DNA proof, so please stop and just tell her the truth. Tara, I am so sorry that I wasn't honest with you. I was trying to protect you."

Mary squeezed her hand and cried. "And I'm so sorry. I never meant to hurt you. I only ever wanted to protect you. Everything I did was from love; you must understand that."

"Mother, you are scaring me. What happened?"

Mary wouldn't make eye contact.

"What happened?" Tara screamed at her.

"I rescued you," Mary said. "I rescued you and brought you here."

"No, no, no," Tara said, her head in her hands. "Why? Why would you do that?"

"Get married, have children, live happily ever after. That's what they told me, but nobody said what to do if the children didn't come. Month after month we hoped and month after month we were let down. For two years we prayed to no avail, no fertility experts back then. With Frank's long hours and me exiled from my job, I was the loneliest I'd ever been.

"When Frank was home, all he spoke of was work. Of this teacher and that, of this child and that. It all sounded the same to me – like wishes that were once mine but were now denied to me.

"It was one of those nights over dinner that he told me of a child in the west countryside who hadn't presented themselves for school. He told me how her father had deserted her mother and rumours were she had turned to the drink. Inspectors and social workers had called to the house many times, but nobody was ever home. All day and night I thought about that little girl. I was tormented. To leave her in that situation was wrong but to take her away was impossible. Don't get me wrong, I would have taken her in a heartbeat, but Frank wasn't keen on adoption or fostering. It was his pride; the local schoolteacher couldn't give his wife a child.

"The following morning, after he left for work, I got in the car and drove west. The roads turned from main to local to lanes to dirt tracks and at the end of one dirt track lined with cornfields there was a rundown house, unsuitable for anyone to live in. I knocked but there was no answer. The side door was open and I thought to take a peek in. I didn't have a plan beyond making sure the little one was okay, but as I entered the house the scream of a new-born pierced the air. Something primal kicked in, something vaster and bigger than me. I followed the scream to a bedroom where a woman lay unresponsive, surrounded by pills and vodka bottles. A tiny pink baby lay naked, its face red from scream-ing, on the bed beside her. I couldn't leave her there.

"I scooped her up and she continued to howl, her flushed body warm and sweaty from the effort. She pushed her thumb into her mouth but that seemed to infuriate her more. The little girl they spoke of was nowhere to be seen, and in that moment, the moment that changed everything, I took her. I took the baby."

She turned to Tara. "I took you."

"No, no, no. You're lying," Tara cried. "Daddy wouldn't have let you. He would have made you bring me back."

"He did," Mary said. "He almost lost his reason. 'Bring that child back to her mother,' he said. I told him your mother was dead. 'She'll be put in the orphanage and you know as well as I do that place is not a good place,' I said.

"'You'll be done for kidnapping,' he said. 'You'll go to prison and my reputation will be ruined.'

"You gulped the bottle of formula I made for you and settled against my chest with a full belly, making those little newborn noises. I was in love with you.

"Frank wanted me to go to the Gardai, tell them your mother was dead, tell them I found you, but you were so content and I persuaded him to let me hold onto you for the night. We both knew when you went back they would put you into care. We both knew what was ahead for you. One night of food and cuddles seemed little to ask.

"The next morning, having not slept a wink, I prepared you to bring back when I switched on the radio and heard the news.

"Your mother had been found dead in her home and Gardai were not treating it as suspicious. Mother of one. It meant they didn't know about you.

"Frank made me swear I would bring the baby back, but the more I spent time with you, I knew I couldn't hand you over to them. I couldn't."

"Why didn't you come back for me?" Cassie asked. "It was me you came for in the first place, why didn't you take me with you?"

"I wasn't thinking straight. We had to move, and quickly, before somebody knew we had the child. We should have come back for you but the longer it went on, the chances of us returning her with no repercussions diminished and the more we lived in fear that someone would find us. Frank took holidays and we upped and left Lenburgh that very night. It was the seventies, it was easy, not like today, all CCTV and internet. It wasn't surprising that people disappeared in the seventies; it was more surprising that they were ever found. People up and moved and never wrote home. Starting a new life, they called it, like when a character leaves a soap opera.

"In a guesthouse by the sea close to here, we listened to every report and read every paper for news of a search for the baby, but there was nothing. By the end of the week, it was pretty clear nobody was coming for you."

Mary paused and looked straight at Cassie. "Frank was worried about you," she told her. "He said you'd surely tell the authorities you had a baby sister and what if you had seen me taking her. But nothing ever came out."

"I saw you that day," Cassie said. "I saw your red car and brown buckled shoes, the ones in that photograph on the wall. I told the police about my baby sister, but they said I was imagining things. They tried to persuade me I was mental, and they nearly did. They said it was damage from finding Mammy dead. But the dreams never stopped and I knew I'd find Tara in the end. At first, I almost felt sorry for you. I thought you bought Tara, like on the news reports, but when I saw the car and your shoes in the picture on the wall, I knew you took her yourself. Wait a minute ..."

Cassie jumped up and Tara grabbed the knife.

"You said our mother was unresponsive when you took Tara."

"No, I said she was dead."

"No, you said she was *unresponsive*. Jesus Christ, she was alive, wasn't she? She was still alive when you took Tara from her arms."

"No, she had overdosed, like it said on the news."

"Was she still breathing?"

"I don't know I – I –"

Cassie swiped the knife from Tara and held it to Mary's throat. "Was she still breathing? Tell me the fucking truth!"

"She wouldn't have made it, even if I'd called for help," Mary cried. "She was dying."

Cassie put her hand over her mouth and fell into a pile on the floor. "Oh my God, you left our mother to die and then you took her child. You killed our mother."

"No, no, it wasn't like that." Mary's breathing was becoming laboured. "No, I did not. She was dying and what sort of a life would Tara have had if I had resuscitated her?

Up on that hill, with you. No, I left her for nature to take its course. I did not kill her." She panted and held her chest.

"Mother, calm yourself," Tara said. "What is it? What's wrong?"

"Leave her," Cassie said. "She's not our mother."

"But she's having a heart attack."

"She's not. That is a lie, too. She's perfectly fine. I called to see her the other day when Doctor Lucas was here. He told her she is making a great recovery, but she never passed that information on, did she?"

"No, she's dying, she is," Tara said.

"Tara, Mary has lied to you your whole life to keep you here with her. Those allergies of yours are as imaginary as that panic attack on your first day of school. She pulled your wings off like a fly she caught and kept you here with her – you may as well have been sitting in that wheelchair with her."

"No, that's not true. I have allergies. Tell her, Mother."

Mary sighed. "I wanted to protect you at all costs. What if you had the allergies? I was terrified to find out, and it didn't harm you, did it?"

"It didn't harm you, but it controlled you. Everything she did was to control you. Nightly dinner, keeping you in that apartment up there, discouraging you from travel or promotions – I mean, it may as well be fucking Rapunzel with her abducting you and keeping you locked in the tower."

Mary gasped for breath. "Help me. Please help me."

"I'll call an ambulance," Tara said.

Cassie stalled for a moment. "We could... or hear me out... what if we don't do anything?"

"She'll die."

"She will. Like our mother died."

Tara's phone rang, making her jump. She glanced at the screen.

"It's Barry," Tara said. "He'll raise the alarm if I don't answer. He knows I'm here."

"Answer it but don't say a word about this or else..."

Tara accepted the call, putting it on speaker.

"Cassie's not here, Tara," Barry shouted over loud background chatter. "I'm calling the police."

"No," Tara replied, "Barry, take the flight! We are completely fine here."

Cassie smiled.

"No way!" Barry said angrily. "I'm not leaving you."

"Please, Barry. It was a huge misunderstanding. Go. I'll fill you in later. I'm fine."

She ended the call, and Cassie snatched the phone away from her. "So, you still want to call the ambulance?"

Mary gasped for air.

"Yes, I do! We have to do something for her."

Cassie laughed. "Why, when you know what she did? She spent her whole life manipulating and controlling you. Wouldn't you like to be in control for once?"

"I can't sit by while she dies!" Tara cried.

"Yes, you can," Cassie replied. "It's completely natural. I mean, not like the movies, but it is as nature intended. Get comfortable, this could take a while."

"How do you know?" Tara's stomach dropped when the realisation hit her. "Oh, no . . . Not Mrs Graham. You killed her?"

"Oh God, Tara, how many times?" Cassie snarled. "That was not my fault. I never laid a finger on her, but I was there when she passed without medical intervention. It was quite beautiful."

Mary's breathing had become more laboured. "Please," she whispered but Cassie refused to act, and instead started rambling about how great life was going to be once Mary was dead.

"Think about it. It will be just us, sisters, like you always wanted. You can give me her house, and I'll continue helping you with your place. I might even get a job if I have a home address. Yeah, I'll get a good job, and you can take the promotion. Go to London, Milan, anywhere you fancy. There'll be nothing holding you back. No more secrets, and no more lies. Just us."

For a brief second, Tara considered how good this would be before shaking herself. "No, it's wrong. She looked after me my whole life. I can't do this to her. Call an ambulance — now!"

Snowy jumped onto the bed, and Cassie grabbed him by the scruff of the neck, then flung him across the room. He hit the wall, squealed, and darted out the door.

Tara couldn't stand it anymore. She lunged at the knife, but Cassie grabbed it first and lashed out, slashing at Tara's upper left arm. Pain sliced through her and warm liquid seeped through her turtleneck. Glancing down, Tara saw a deep cut below her bicep and felt like she might pass out.

"Why did you make me do that?" Cassie cried. "You're ruining everything."

"Call 999!"

Cassie paced. "No. Nobody leaves or enters until she's dead. We agreed."

"I did not agree to that! Look at me, Cassie! I need medical attention."

"And we'll get it. Just not yet. Tie something around your arm."

"There are sheets up there," Tara said, indicating to the high shelves by the open door. "Let me get one."

Cassie glanced from the shelves to Tara, and back again. "I'll get it," she said, and reached up. Tara took her chance, running for the bedroom door, but with an almighty yank Cassie pulled her backwards by the hair. Turning, she saw Cassie looming over her, her eyes dark, the knife raised. "You stupid bitch!"

Tara closed her eyes, bracing herself, when suddenly Cassie shrieked. Tara opened her eyes to see Barry pinning Cassie to the ground. Behind him, police officers filled the room, and took over.

Barry stumbled to his feet, panting, then turned to Tara. "Are you okay? Jesus, your arm!"

"She stabbed me!"

"Why?" Cassie cried at Barry, while her hands were cuffed behind her back. "Why did you come? She said she was fine!"

Barry cradled Tara. "Correct. That's exactly what she said. Fine. Although I was already on my way at that point. There was no way I was leaving the country with all this going on."

Fine. Their codeword, and the spare key — all part of the plan. Tara's plan.

***

Two paramedics loaded Mary into an ambulance, an oxygen mask covering her tiny face.

"Will she be okay?" Tara asked, holding her arm, now bound tightly.

"She's in good hands," one of them answered. "You need to come too. That arm needs urgent attention."

When Tara stepped into the ambulance, over forty years

of lies, and deceit flooded her brain. She stepped back out, and looked at Barry. "Will you take me instead?"

"Of course," he said, "but don't you want to go with your mother?"

"No, thanks, I'll travel separately. Besides, she's not my mother."

36

CASSIE

One year later

Cassie joined the queue for the phone. The prison staff were kind, but firm. As long as the residents caused no trouble, and played by the rules, they had no issue. Cassie kept herself to herself. She'd been in the game long enough to know to be friendly, but not befriend, to trust, but not get close. Letting others in only ever ended in getting burned, and Cassie had enough hurt to last her a lifetime. Besides, they may have been in the same situation, but there were no besties in this dog-eat-dog world. A world where you could lose your teeth over a simple misunderstanding.

It wasn't that she was scared. Cassie was no coward, and had been well able to look out for herself since childhood. But she was cautious.

Self-preservation from necessity, Sharon had called it.

She'd been sentenced to fifteen months for assault, better than eleven years for attempted murder, dodged thanks to Tara's interjection on her behalf. It wasn't fair, though. Anyone would have reacted in the same way to discovering their mother was murdered. It wasn't her fault.

Cassie's life should have been different. She shouldn't have been here in this place with nothing to call her own, but, no matter how hard she tried, it was always one step forward, two steps back. People saw what they wanted to see; she never stood a chance. She was a fool to believe false claims of care, and fondness. She'd let her guard down, but she wouldn't let it happen again. No, Cassie managed better in this world with just herself to look after, and just herself to let down. From here on in, she was going to look out for number one.

She reached the top of the queue, inserted her coins into the payphone, and dialled Tara's number.

EPILOGUE
TARA

"Come on up." Her suitcase stood waiting at the door of her apartment, passport and plane tickets on top.

She left the door ajar, and did her final checks. Bills paid, fridge empty, no business left unfinished. Her gaze shifted to the pile of unopened letters on the counter, marked Lap of Luxury Residential Home.

Mary had survived the ordeal, but the delay in seeking help had left her with complex medical needs, and residential care was the logical solution. Tara sold Mary's house, paid for a luxurious nursing home, and then left her there. She never went back, despite the constant requests for visits, despite letters every week. Her conscience was quite clear over that.

"You ready?" Barry stuck his head in the door.

She laughed with happiness. "Absolutely! Hey, have you been crying?"

He chuckled. "Ah, don't mind me. I'm just happy for you.

Getting to spread your wings at last — Paris, Rome, Amsterdam — and I get to be a part of it."

Tara pulled him into a hug. "Thank you. For everything. I couldn't do it without you... who else would look after these three while I'm gone?" The cats languished on the couch, unfazed, and like they owned the place. "Oh, and you have all the codes for this place, right?"

Barry saluted, making her laugh. "Aye, aye captain. Are you absolutely sure you want to go alone?"

"Positive. I need to this for myself." She inhaled deeply, scanning the apartment one last time, while Barry wheeled her case into the tiny corridor. The curtains! She hurried across the apartment to close them, stopping dead at the sight of Mary's old house. The new owners were renovating, and the whole back of the house had been ripped off, exposing the old living room wallpaper.

Tara pet, I'd be lost without you.

Her phone rang, and she knew who it was without checking. Cassie. Tara had promised she would help her get on her feet when she was released. There was money in the bank, and she was her sister after all.

"Are you going to answer that?" Barry asked.

Cassie phoned on the same day every week, but over time her calls had become rants of self-pity, with what she said on one call contradicting another. She never asked about Tara, and frankly, Tara had no interest in having a relationship with her. That ship had sailed, along with her regular wine o'clock. She was not an alcoholic, despite what Cassie insisted. She was nothing like her. Nothing.

Barry joined her at the window. "Are you okay?"

She rejected the call, and drew the curtains. "I'm fine. No, I'm more than fine. I'm free."

ACKNOWLEDGMENTS

To Brian Lynch and all at Inkubator Books, I'm incredibly fortunate to work with you. Thanks Alice Latchford for your story edits, support, and guidance. You made it fun. Thanks to Emma Hargrave for editing and Debs Warner for proofreading. Also, thanks to Claire Milto and the team at Inkubator for making the whole process so enjoyable.

Thanks to the staff in Mullingar Library for letting me hang out while writing this book.

Big thanks to those who answered my million questions, in particular Amie Connor, Ger McAuley, Brian McLoughlin, and Claire Butler.

Thanks to my parents, family, and friends for all the encouragement and to Brendan for waiting patiently on the first million.

And finally to you, the reader. Of all the books in all the world you chose this one and I am so grateful you did. I hope we meet again very soon.

If you could leave a review of *Be Careful What You Wish For* on Amazon and Goodreads, I would be so grateful. It helps smashing readers like you find the book.

ABOUT THE AUTHOR

Lorraine Murphy takes everyday situations and twists them into terrifying tales. She is the author of Into the Woods and numerous published, and winning, flash fiction stories.

A software engineer by profession, she's had many careers including slimming club leader, adult educator, charity co-founder, chairperson, activist and entrepreneur. As a teenager, she adored Stephen King and later found herself on the jury of an infamous murder trial.

When she's not writing, Lorraine is always into something, whether it be competing in/ for her local Toastmasters club or jumping out of a fully functional airplane. She lives in Westmeath, Ireland with her husband Brendan and three taller children.

www.lorraineamurphy.com

ALSO BY LORRAINE MURPHY

Into the Woods

Be Careful What You Wish For

Printed in Great Britain
by Amazon